SINGLE SICKNESS

SINGLE SICKNESS
and other stories
by Masuda Mizuko

TRANSLATED BY

LYNNE KUTSUKAKE

∾

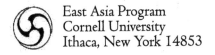
East Asia Program
Cornell University
Ithaca, New York 14853

The Cornell East Asia Series is published by the Cornell University East Asia Program (distinct from Cornell University Press). We publish books on a variety of scholarly topics relating to East Asia as a service to the academic community and the general public. Standing Orders, which provide for automatic notification and invoicing of each title in the series upon publication, are accepted.

Address submission inquiries to CEAS Editorial Board, East Asia Program, Cornell University, 140 Uris Hall, Ithaca New York 14853-7601.

Cover concept and book layout: Mai
Cover image: Image of "Woman in the Rain" only, created by Rafal Cichowski (Vincent Noir). Used with permission from the artist.

Number 156 in the Cornell East Asia Series.
New Japanese Horizon Series Editors: Michiko Wilson/Gustav Heldt/Doug Merwin
Originally published in Japanese. Copyright Kemuri ©1997 / Mizu ©1997 / Dokushinbyō ©1983 / Tsuno ©1997 / Kagami ©1997 / Jikan ©1997 / Yumenmushi ©1991. All by Masuda Mizuko.
Copyright English language translations ©2011 by Lynne Kutsukake. All rights reserved.
ISSN: 1050-2955
ISBN: 978-1-933947-26-6 hardcover
ISBN: 978-1-933947-56-3 paperback
Library of Congress Control Number: 2011935433
25 24 22 22 21 20 19 18 17 16 15 14 13 12 11   9 8 7 6 5 4 3 2 1

∞ The paper in this book meets the requirements for permanence of ISO 9706:1994.

Contents

~

Acknowledgments

⁓

For their enthusiastic support, wise guidance and many acts of kindness, I would like to thank Ted Goossen, Miya Narushima, Sonja Arntzen, Atsuko Sakaki, Sarah Strong, Susie Schmidt, Kim Kyong Suk and my husband Michael Donnelly. I would also like to thank the anonymous reader for several helpful suggestions. Any errors or omissions are, of course, entirely my responsibility.

I am very grateful to Michiko Wilson, editor of the Japanese Horizons series, for selecting my manuscript. Heartfelt thanks to Mai Shaikhanuar-Cota, managing editor of CEAS, for working so hard to bring this book to press.

Finally, I would like to express my deep gratitude to the author, Masuda Mizuko, for her generous cooperation with this project and her everlasting patience. I hope I have done justice to her writing.

Introduction

∾

Masuda Mizuko (1948–) first came to the attention of Japan's literary community when her novella, "Posthumous Ties" (Shigo no Kankei, 1977), was shortlisted for the Shincho Prize for New Writers. The noted critic Akiyama Shun enthusiastically welcomed Masuda's debut. Her writing, he declared, "marked the appearance of an entirely new individuality."[1] In "Posthumous Ties," Masuda probed with fierce intensity the relationship of the individual to the group, in this case, the relationship of a female student to a group of male student activists on a college campus. The tensions arising between the individual and the community—between self and other(s)—would become a central thematic thread running throughout Masuda's subsequent writing.

In the following six years, between 1978 and 1983, Masuda received a total of six nominations for the prestigious Akutagawa Prize for "Key to a room for one" ("Koshitsu no kagi," 1978), Sakura dormitory ("Sakuraryō," 1978), "Two springs" ("Futatsu

---

1 Akiyama Shun reaffirmed his endorsement of Masuda's writing in the kaisetsu he wrote for the paperback edition of the short story collection *Futatsu no haru*, which includes "Posthumous Ties." See "Kaisetsu," *Futatsu no haru*. (Fukutake bunko). Tōkyō: Fukutake Shoten, 1986, 298–306.

no haru," 1979), "Until the memorial service" ("Ireisai made," 1979), "A little prostitute" ("Chiisa na shōfu," 1981), and "A modest night scene" ("Uchiki na yakei," 1983). Since then she has been the recipient of numerous literary awards: the Noma New Writers Award in 1984 for *Free Time* (*Jiyū jikan*), the Izumi Kyōka Prize in 1986 for *Single Cell* (*Shinguru seru*), the Ministry of Education Fine Arts Award in 1992 for *Dream Bug* (*Yumenmushi*), and the Itō Sei Literary Prize in 2001 for *Moonviewing* (*Tsukuyomi*).

Masuda Mizuko was born on November 13, 1948, in Tokyo into a middle-class family, the second of three children. She grew up in the Shitamachi area of Tokyo, and the physical geography and civic space of the city—especially the area around the Sumida River—figure largely in her writing, as background locales and as representations of mind-states and being. From the time she was a child, gender issues appear to have had a strong impact on her. As a self-proclaimed tomboy, she was active in track and field and other sports, and considered herself no different from her older brother, but upon entering middle school, she experienced what she has characterized as her first major setback (*zasetsu*)—being forced to wear a skirt. It was part of her new mandatory school uniform. No matter how much she protested about the skirt, no one would take her seriously and she was labeled a "peculiar girl." Later she would confess that for some reason as a child she had simply assumed she would grow up to be a man. The realization that this wasn't going to happen came to her as a huge disappointment. "I simply couldn't believe that I didn't have the right to choose my gender," she wrote in *Flight from Womanhood* (*Onna kara no tōsō*, 1986).[2]

Masuda's rebellious streak persisted well into adolescence. Although she was successful in gaining admission to a prestigious

---

2 Masuda Mizuko. "Onna to iu mono wa ...," *Onna kara no tōsō*. Tōkyō: Kayōsha, 1986, 27–31.

high school, she became so disillusioned with the competitive atmosphere that she dropped out after only one year. Not long after, she resumed her education at a different school, this time as a part-time student. By now she was writing poetry. Before she turned eighteen, she had published her first poem.

Masuda went on to study at Tokyo University of Agriculture and Technology (Tōkyō Nōkō Daigaku), where she majored in biology, specializing in plant immunology. Her decision to study science was an interesting choice, especially given the fact that she was already writing and publishing poetry and had from an early age demonstrated strong leanings towards literature, history and philosophy, areas in which she read voraciously and eclectically. When, in an interview with Kōno Taeko, she was asked why she chose to study science rather than the humanities, Masuda explained that she had always been fascinated by the mystery of life (*seimei*) and felt that science was the best way to understand its fundamental essence.[3] What did it mean to be alive? What did it mean to be a human being? One might even say that she sought to apply the logic and precision of scientific analysis to an intensely personal philosophical quest.

The influence of science can be seen throughout Masuda's writing in her spare, detached style, the neutral observant eye, and the subject matter she favors. Her interest in how biological principles extend to human relations and her keen attention to the physical composition of the body and the natural world seem to be clearly rooted in this early grounding in the sciences.

Masuda attended university during the final years of the turbulent student movement. Perhaps because she was slightly

---

3 Kōno Taeko and Masuda Mizuko. "Taidan Mugibue o megutte," *Mugibue.* (Fukutake bunko). Fukutake Shoten, 1986, 290–311.

older than the average college freshman or perhaps because of her deeply independent nature, her perspective on student politics was refreshingly cynical and tart. In "Posthumous Ties," the apolitical protagonist Keiko has a short, mainly sexual, relationship with a prominent leader in the student movement. He commits suicide, and after his death, Keiko is made the convenient scapegoat by his followers who accuse her of goading him into self-destruction. As a character, Keiko bears many features that would become hallmarks of other female figures who populate the Masuda world. She is single—independent, unencumbered, but also isolated. She is a sexual being whose sexuality is a target of criticism because it is solely for selfish pleasure without goals of reproduction or service within a domestic unit. And she is thoroughly unsentimental, without any trace of a nurturing, romantic nature. It is these aspects of Keiko's character that so enrage the male friends of her former boyfriend and make them want to vilify her.

While Masuda's reputation was steadily growing in critical circles, it was the publication of her novel *Single Cell* in 1986, winner of that year's prestigious Izumi Kyoka Prize, which catapulted her into the broader public limelight. By telling the story of a lonely insecure graduate student who tries but ultimately fails to make a connection with a young woman—another "single cell" like himself—the novel seemed to tap directly into the zeitgeist of Japan's modern urban youth. Masuda's trope of the single cell draws upon an actual scientific fact. It is a fundamental principle in biology that cells will naturally gravitate towards each other in order to form a larger organism. Single cells—cells that remain unattached and are capable of surviving on their own—are considered to be rare and unnatural occurrences, not the norm. In Masuda's fictional world, however, contemporary society is increasingly populated by these anomalous single cells.

With the publication of *Single Cell*, the word "single" came to be seen as a kind of signature keyword for Masuda. In her afterword to the novel, she wrote that she liked the title very much, and even thought that "single cell" would have been just as appropriate for her two preceding novels *Straw Whistle* (*Mugibue*, 1981) and *Free Time* (*Jiyū jikan*, 1984). She went on to explain that although she might appear to be unduly fixated on the theme of "singlehood," it was because she believed that people were best understood if examined as individuals, not as part of a group.[4] Indeed, Masuda's focus is invariably trained on the *kojin*—the individual—set against or apart from the *kyōdōtai*—the community. While the "single" of *Single Cell* is a metaphor for the essential aloneness of the individual and the inescapable separation of self from other, "single" also connotes independence, autonomy, and singularity. Especially as expressed in the lives of Masuda's female characters, singlehood, whether by deliberate choice or not, also implies a critique of conventional domestic values concerning family and male-female relationships.

Many of the characters in Masuda's oeuvre are single women who seek to establish the boundaries of the self against the social expectations of the larger systems or organizations of which they are part. At the same time, they want to balance the autonomy of independent selfhood against the loneliness of the solitary life. The stories in this collection feature a range of characters—all but one are single and all but one are women—who face these challenges in various ways.

Published in 1981, "Single Sickness" is an example of an early Masuda story. After graduating from university with a degree in biology, Masuda worked for almost eight years as a research

---

4 Masuda's comments appear in her afterword to the paperback edition of *Single Cell*. Tōkyō: Fukutake Shoten, 1988, 266. For an English language introduction to *Single Cell*, see the Japan P.E.N. Club essay translated by Mark Jewel in *Japanese Literature Today*, 13 (1988), 14–15.

assistant at Nippon Medical School (Nihon Ika Daigaku), and the setting of "Single Sickness" is one she knew intimately. Fukue, the unmarried cancer researcher, may be a professional scientist but her status in the research institute is undermined at every turn by her sex. She is ridiculed by her male colleagues, and forced to conduct her work in isolation and without support. She feels stuck at the institute, believing that it is impossible to find another position elsewhere. Her state of inertia and emotional "singleness" is finally challenged by an unexpected health crisis. Ironically, Fukue, the scientist, who has worked so hard to reproduce cancer cells in her lab mice, finds that Fukue, the woman, has developed a lump in her breast.

Fukue assumes that she has cancer and her fears prompt her to consider the nature of what it means to be a woman. What function do these breasts serve, she wants to know. Why does she have to have them if they are going to cause disease, even death. The doctor who informs Fukue that what she has is mastitis is the embodiment of male arrogance. He insinuates that she has brought this condition on herself by not fulfilling her duties as a female. Her breasts were meant to produce milk, and by not marrying and becoming a mother, she has denied this part of her body the opportunity to perform its assigned scientific function. Even the cancer-riddled lab mouse is pregnant. When Fukue performs an autopsy on the animal, she discovers its womb is full of tiny fetuses. Only by fleeing the poisonous environment of the male research institute is Fukue finally able to achieve freedom.

The single woman in Masuda's fiction is a figure who subverts the traditional values of marriage, family and the home, not because of anything she does but simply because of who she is, and what she is not—that is, not married or not part of a family.

Fukue is an example of one of Masuda's many single, independent working women who are able to support themselves economically, however modestly. For the most part, they are ordinary and unassuming, scarcely firebrand feminists with political agendas. But in a society driven by myths of matrimony and maternity, the very act of being single represents an affront to unquestioned assumptions about the desirability of marriage, domesticity, and even romantic love. To be a single cell is to fundamentally disrupt the stability of existing social systems and constructs.

Ginko in "Smoke"[5] was once married to a man of questionable character who simply vanished one day, leaving her alone. In her case, the desertion comes as a relief. Not only does she not know exactly what prompted her to get married in the first place, she is not even sure who she married. For Ginko, going back to being single means returning to a more natural state than the state of matrimony. Given her suspicions of her ex-husband's potential for deception and violence, one can hardly blame her for feeling as she does.

This story also develops a theme which runs throughout the collection; that is, the underlying sense of menace in everyday mundane existence and the unforeseen danger that lurks in the realm of the domestic. After Ginko is knocked down the stairs in her condominium building by a threatening stranger, what does she do to calm herself? She engages in housework. But the domestic activity she undertakes—collecting the garbage in her apartment—ends up triggering unexpected memories and bringing buried emotions to the fore. When she turns on the television, she learns about a murder victim whose body parts were cut up and disposed of in garbage bags similar to the kind

---

5 My translation originally appeared under the title "Where There's Smoke" in *Japanese Language and Literature*, 38 (2004), 57–79.

she is using. Furthermore, she is reminded of a recent case in which a man murdered his wife and small children and stuffed their bodies into garbage bags he found in the kitchen. Ginko cannot help thinking about how it was probably the man's wife who, in her housewifely duties, had purchased the bags. Ginko's ruminations ultimately lead her to recall the discomfort of her own marriage and to understand that the generalized anxiety she had always felt about her ex-husband was actually genuine fear—fear of a man she could never really comprehend or guess what he was capable of. Taken to extremes, one might say that the most dangerous place for a woman to be is in a marriage. Small wonder that so many Masuda characters prefer to stay single.

"Smoke," "Water," "Horn," "Time," and "Mirror" are taken from the loosely linked short story collection Water Mirror (Mizu kagami, 1997). Despite different main characters, subtle references to similar figures and violent incidents recur and the stories effectively evoke a sense of danger and fear lurking in encounters between men and women. In "Mirror," a middle-aged single woman is pushed off an embankment by an unknown assailant. By the end of the story, she learns that the young nurse in the hospital where she has been recovering was murdered by her boyfriend. In "Time," the first half of the story is taken up with Kasumi's efforts to escape the harassment of a former lover, a man who fills her with so much revulsion she feels she could kill him. She marries an old friend (is it in part to get as far away as possible from the hated ex-lover?) and even in her marriage she continues to live as if she were still alone, spending most of her time by herself in the claustrophobic confines of the apartment, which, her husband believes, is haunted by the ghost of his now dead ex-fiancee. In "Water," Ikuri is young, single and supposedly free to do whatever she wants, but she finds that her plans start to unravel when a water leak brings her into conflict with her belligerent male neighbor. The flood of water, like the bursting of emotional dams, is terrifying for her, a threat to the integrity of her selfhood. It breaks down the very structure of her home, the carapace she has so determinedly erected as a shelter for the self she would create. Masuda taps into a dark undercurrent of disquiet in the lives of her characters who are nervous and edgy no matter where they are. Even in the privacy of one's own home, it is hard to feel safe. Singlehood, it is clear, cannot shelter one completely from the anxieties and disappointments of modern life.

In several of the stories, the female body undergoes imaginative transformations: A horn sprouts on a woman's forehead (in "Horn"); a tumor may or may not be secretly growing inside a breast (in "Single Sickness"); a woman can't get rid of the athlete's foot she contracted from a former lover (in "Time"); bodies are cut up into pieces and stuffed in garbage bags for easier disposal (in "Smoke"). This gaze upon the body is by turns clinical, humorous, and morbid. The middle-aged female narrator of "Horn" begins by recounting the changes in her body with droll bemusement. Unmarried and employed in a dull job working for the city parks department where she dispenses gardening advice, the narrator has no explanation for why a horn should suddenly have begun to grow in the middle of her forehead. She monitors its development with ghoulish fascination, taking precise scientific measurements of size and color and noting the occult-like powers it seems to be giving her. She states with confidence that it cannot be a secondary sexual characteristic because of her age—she is already way too old for that. As the horn grows, it becomes more conspicuous. She waits with a mixture of anticipation and dread to see what will happen when her co-workers notice.

"Horn" may be read as a contemporary parody of the *yamanba* tale, the myth of the old hag with demonic powers. Yet, while the narrator discovers that the horn gives her the ability to read minds, the thoughts of others are so petty and mean-spirited she honestly wishes she didn't have such powers. As a middle-aged never-been-married woman—an old maid—the narrator occupies a class of women who have been rendered virtually invisible to the rest of society. She is of little or no consequence to the people around her. Although her colleagues eventually notice the deformity on her forehead and have a heated discussion about whether it really qualifies as a horn, not even something as radical as sprouting a horn is enough to engage their sustained attention and concern. They are momentarily curious about her because having a horn gives her the status of a freak. But, in fact, as an older unmarriageable woman, she was already a kind of freak to them anyway.

"Dream Bug" differs from the other stories in having a male protagonist. The college-age Hideo is adrift, not yet as independent from his family as he would like to be but emotionally distant from all the values espoused by his father. He finds an odd soulmate in his deceased uncle, a man he never knew and whose very existence seems to have been an embarrassment to the rest of the family. Hideo's obsession with Katsuzo develops into an intense identification, to the point where he feels that going into his uncle's deserted coffee shop is like "entering the body of a dead person." The coffee shop is located in a dingy, untraveled section of Shitamachi, a place frozen in time and somehow forgotten by modern developments. Entering the coffee shop allows Hideo to travel back in his own private time, to remember the past and to come to an understanding of its impact on him. In his conflicted desires—for anonymity and freedom from the demands of family on the one hand and for deep connection and love on the other—Masuda poignantly captures essential facets of the complex human condition.

The stories in this collection provide only a sampling of Masuda's writing, but I hope that through this publication another distinctive voice has been added to the growing corpus of Japanese women writers available in English. My own discovery of Masuda's fiction was, in fact, through translation. I came upon two intriguing short stories, both wonderfully translated into English—one by Yukiko Tanaka ("Sinking ground") and another by Seiji Lippit ("Living alone")—and they whet my appetite to read more of this author.[6] As there were no other works available in English, I sought out the original Japanese. The act of reading a work of fiction involves entering a unique imaginative world—turn to the first page, begin reading and let yourself be drawn into another subjectivity. Without translation, however, the door to that imaginative world is locked to readers who lack the key of language. I am grateful to the New Japanese Horizons translation series and the Cornell East Asia Series for strong commitment to translations and to bringing new Japanese voices to new readers.

∾

---

6 "Sinking ground" (Chinka chitai), translated by Yukiko Tanaka, *Unmapped Territories: New Women's Fiction from Japan* (Seattle: Women in Translation, 1991), 39–68. "Living alone" (Hitorigurashi), translated by Seiji M. Lippit, *Review of Japanese Culture and Society*, 2(1) (1988), 77–91.

Smoke

Ginko left work a little earlier than usual. When she arrived at her station, she took the long way home past the pharmacy where she bought garbage bags and bath soap. She knew the man behind the cash register—the pharmacist—by sight. "Take good care of yourself!" he said in a bright cheery voice when he handed Ginko her change and the bag containing her purchases. Clad in his ubiquitous white lab coat, the pharmacist loved dispensing advice about medications, so whenever a customer asked a question the line-up at the cash register would grow quite long. No matter what a customer bought, the pharmacist always smiled and said, "Take good care of yourself!" He would follow this up with the words "Please come again" addressed to the back of the departing customer as he or she stepped out of the store. His timing of these two refrains was perfect.

Something rather unpleasant had happened earlier at the office, and Ginko wasn't feeling in top form. In fact just as the pharmacist delivered his "Take good care of yourself!" she remembered that she needed something for her headache. She was about to turn around and go back for it when the pharmacist followed up with the usual "Please come again." Looking at the line-up that had formed at the cash register, Ginko decided to forget it. Leaving the pharmacy she marched straight down the main avenue and into Maruetsu Supermarket. As she had originally planned, she went up to the drug counter on the second floor and bought some painkillers. The druggist here was a taciturn older woman who bowed her head formally, "Thank you for your patronage." Just that. She never wasted any extra words, never offered anything like "Take care of yourself" or "Hope you're feeling better soon."

Ginko liked to divide her shopping between the two places, not out of any preference for the service she received but in order to save money: she bought her household necessities and artificial sweetener at the pharmacy and her medicine at the second-floor drug counter in the supermarket because it worked out cheaper that way. Today in particular Ginko wished she could get the older woman to say something more personal. "I can't seem to get rid of this headache," she ventured as she gathered up her purchase. The druggist looked at Ginko sympathetically. "Thank you for your patronage," she repeated in the next breath. Not only was it disappointing, Ginko felt cheated for the effort she'd made. As she left she heard the druggist's tiny voice saying thank you yet again.

Garbage bags were tucked in a corner of the supermarket on the first floor. Ginko checked the price. Yes, the pharmacy was indeed a lot cheaper! This lifted her mood considerably and she resolved to inquire about the price of headache medication the next time she was there.

The painkillers were for the dull headache that had been dogging her all day ever since her boss had approached her again on the matter of a transfer. His voice had been dripping with sarcasm. "Granted being married makes things hard, I know, but if you don't accept other postings, you can't expect to be promoted. Or is living apart for this assignment going to be a problem?"

None of his damned business! For the past few years, whenever a transfer was offered, as it was almost every year, Ginko managed to turn it down. Perhaps because of this she had now come under special scrutiny. But Ginko felt no desire to move whatsoever. She liked her life just as it was: the condominium she had bought on her own, the routine of commuting back and forth to her government job as she had for the past ten years. The thought of moving to a strange place filled her with anxiety.

"Stupid!" she muttered aloud to no one in particular as she stepped out of the supermarket. That made her feel better. It was a beautiful day. When the weather was so fine, the sky appeared higher, the world more spacious and wide.

There was a shortcut to her apartment through the back entrance of the condominium and up the stairs to the third floor. Pushing open the heavy steel door to the stairwell, Ginko stepped inside out of the light. Once the door had closed behind her, she was plunged into murky darkness and felt the cool damp air caress her cheeks. She was aware of her headache forming a hard ball in the center of her head.

Her shoes made a noisy scuffling sound on the concrete steps as she began to climb. Suddenly she heard a loud bang overhead. A large man in a suit shot out from the second floor doorway and started racing down the stairs, looking back over his shoulder as he ran. Ginko made a flustered attempt to step out of his way, but everything happened too fast. The man slammed full steam into her with a force so hard she was knocked off her feet and sent flying down the stairs. The next thing she knew her body was splayed awkwardly across the cold concrete landing. Granted she wasn't unconscious, but she'd received a hard blow to the hip. The pain was so sharp she could hardly breathe, let alone move.

The large man came and stood directly over her. He didn't look at all sorry for what he had done, merely annoyed. When Ginko's eyes met his, he shifted his gaze away, extracted a cigarette from his suit pocket and proceeded to light it. Meanwhile Ginko patted different parts of her body, trying to determine if she'd been injured. There was no blood, nor did she appear to have broken any bones, but her body was hot, perhaps from agitation. Slowly she stood up and gingerly tested one foot, then the other. Everything seemed alright. Puffing on his cigarette, the man watched her every movement intently. His silence gave her the creeps but she wasn't about to be the first to speak. The man was young, probably in his twenties, with a pudgy baby face that didn't match his brazen insolence. He showed no emotion, and it was impossible for her to tell what might be going through his head.

Ginko set about gathering up her scattered things, but the man made no move to help. As she bent over, he let the ash from his cigarette drop just inches from her face. What if he's some kind of deviant, she suddenly thought. Genuinely frightened now, she quickly looked up, this time to meet the man's eyes directly. He pinched the cigarette between his fingers and slowly took it from his mouth. Taking aim at Ginko's face, he suddenly expelled a huge lungful of smoke. The attack was so unexpected, she was overcome by a violent bout of coughing. Then she heard an odd staccato sound: why, the man was laughing! Before Ginko even had time to be surprised, he bounded down the stairs at lightning speed. The outer door slammed shut with a loud heavy crash. With the man's departure, the stairwell was once again absolutely still. Clutching her garbage bags, soap, and handbag to her breast, Ginko stood frozen to the spot, stunned. What the hell are you doing! Stupid! Look out, you idiot! Watch where you're going! The words came tumbling out under her breath.

Rushing to her apartment, she locked the door and drew the chain. She flung her purchases on the kitchen table. Grabbing a tissue she wiped her tear-filled eyes, then threw back a couple of painkillers with a cup of water. Her hip throbbed from her fall and her ankles and elbows were smarting. Who the hell was that man! But how could she possibly know? She'd never seen him in the building before. The only thing she knew for certain was that he'd come running out from the second floor, but most of the apartments on that floor were rented out as office space, so all kinds of people went in and out. Clearly this guy was a cheap punk, trying to make a fast getaway from whatever mischief he'd been up to in one of the offices. Yet the fact that he had waited around until he was sure Ginko wasn't seriously injured showed some small, quite unexpected, measure of decency. She emitted a hollow, dry cough. The smoke he had blown into her face seemed to have penetrated deep down her windpipe making it tight and sore, and coughing brought tears to her eyes. She felt truly miserable.

It's when you're down that the worst things happen, she thought, recalling an incident from long ago. She had gone to check the entrance exam results for her first choice university only to find that her name wasn't on the list of successful applicants. Then on her way home on the train she'd encountered a pervert. She was sunk into a seat on the train, absorbed in her disappointment, when a man came and stood right in front of her. Glancing up, she noticed he was smirking at her. He then leaned forward, draping himself over her, and let the front of his coat fall open. Underneath he was stark naked. The moment Ginko raised her head, the man flashed a broad grin as if he had been waiting for just this opportunity. He made no move to leave. At the next station Ginko leapt up and fled the train. When she glanced back, the pervert was looking straight at her and waving his hand.

All garbage bags sold in the City now contained calcium carbonate, as per Tokyo municipal government regulations. It gave the bags an unpleasant rough texture, and when Ginko cut open the package she had purchased, just touching the bags brought goose pimples to her flesh. Beginning in January 1994 it was decreed that garbage would not be collected unless it was packed in the new semi-transparent "calcium carbonate" bags which all residents would now have to purchase. The City claimed that the new garbage bags reduced damage to its incinerators because calcium carbonate prevented sudden rises in temperature in the burning process. This view was challenged by the "anti" group for whom the benefits of calcium carbonate were questionable: in their opinion it increased ash production and was uneconomical to boot. But the opposition was swiftly and summarily crushed, and the City got its way. A government bureaucrat herself, Ginko was relieved that she worked for the national, not the municipal, government, and had had nothing to do with these bags. Of course, she threw out garbage too. If she wanted it picked up, like everyone else she had to buy the new bags.

In Ginko's view, mixing calcium carbonate into garbage bags was a colossal waste of time and energy. Wouldn't it have been simpler to shovel the calcium carbonate directly into the City incinerators and save everybody the trouble of manufacturing, purchasing, and burning the darn bags? But, of course, there were always other considerations. As a civil servant, Ginko was only too familiar with the reams of paperwork and bureaucratic reports that had to accompany every stage of a new project from its inception to final implementation, and she knew how impossible it was to make changes mid-stream.

As she had already opened the package of garbage bags, she went around her apartment collecting refuse. Still reeling from the shock of the stairwell incident, she felt the need to occupy herself—to do something, anything. But with a capacity of twelve gallons, the bag was huge, and try as she might, she never had enough garbage to fill it. Whenever she opened a new bag, Ginko was seized by a desire to stuff it to the brim. On occasion she had tossed in old newspapers and even empty boxes, but never once had she managed to fill the whole thing. With collection three times a week, there simply wasn't enough garbage.

She stared at the bag in her hands, still flat and limp. Abruptly she lifted one foot and inserted it into the bag. Then she followed with the other foot. Holding the mouth of the bag up at the sides, she gently eased her hips down to the bottom. Ginko was a small woman and by squatting down in the bag she found it covered her completely up to her neck. Although she hated touching the bags, being inside one was a different matter. Except for the tickling of paper scraps between her legs, the feeling of being enclosed was surprisingly nice. Her lower body grew warm, all tension melted away.

Ginko got out of the bag, emptied the garbage, and then climbed back inside again. She scrunched her body as small as she could make it, and by pushing upwards managed to stretch the bag till it formed pleats around her neck. But there was simply no way of getting it over her head. She had no choice. Once more she stepped out of the bag and plucked another one from the package. It was tricky navigating her way through the scattered refuse. Why hadn't she transferred the garbage into a new bag instead of dumping it on the floor? For that matter, why hadn't she just used a new bag? It made her a little uneasy to see herself throwing trash on the floor and climbing into garbage bags, but she did not want to stop. Anyway, who was she harming? Eventually she would pick everything up off the floor and take her garbage out as usual. In the meantime why couldn't she do whatever she wanted with these brand new bags she'd bought and paid for herself.

She climbed back into the first bag and pulled the new one over her head. Then she tugged the bottom bag up and the top one down as far as they would go.

Semi-transparent my eye, thought Ginko. You can't see a thing. Aside from some green lettering stamped on the bag itself—"City of Tokyo Approved"—all she could make out was the hazy glow of her lamp. Inside the bags it was bright. A pleasant, comforting brightness. Wrapped in this soothing warmth and quiet, she grew sleepy. Finally, she felt safe.

The purpose of making the garbage bags semi-transparent was to allow for the ready examination and identification of their contents. Had the garbage been properly separated according to municipal garbage regulations? Did it contain any dangerous or toxic items? Yet from inside Ginko couldn't see anything, not even the furniture in the room. Just how transparent were these bags? If she remained perfectly motionless, could someone looking at this bag tell there was a body inside? Would he or she know right away that it was Ginko?

What the hell am I doing? Ginko muttered to herself a few moments later. Her head felt as woolly as if she had been asleep. Still she made no move to get out of the bags, which were curiously comfortable. She'd probably been sitting as she was for at least five minutes, but there was no way of being sure since she couldn't see the clock. Anyway if she fell fast asleep just like this, who was there to object? Maybe before, her husband might have said something, but he wasn't around anymore. In any case, her sitting inside garbage bags and her husband were two completely separate things—they had nothing to do with each other. Just as Ginko and her husband had nothing to do with each other.

Her breath made a soft swooshing sound and hit the side of

the bags with a hefty whoomp. The bags quivered slightly with each inhalation and exhalation. After the warm air hit the side, it slid down to the bottom where it pooled. Ginko's lower body grew hot and she felt like she was on the verge of falling asleep. She opened and shut her eyes in time with her breathing. Yet even when she closed her eyes, it did not become totally dark: the field of white before her simply blurred and drifted farther away. When she opened her eyes, a white wall shot towards her.

Ginko's breathing wheezed like rushing wind. Although it sounded labored, in fact she did not feel it was getting any more difficult to breathe. Still, a plastic bag was a plastic bag, whether or not it contained calcium carbonate: presumably if you kept one over your head long enough, you would suffocate. A distinction was made between regular polyvinyl bags that were used for disposing of "nonburnable" garbage and calcium carbonate bags which were strictly for "burnable." Given their flimsy, papery feel, she wondered if the bags she was sitting in were ever so slightly porous. She wished she could tie the bags tightly shut with string and sit still inside for hours on end.

As she got hotter and hotter, Ginko was struck by the sudden urge to take off her clothes and sit inside the bags stark naked. Wouldn't that feel wonderful! Reflected against the milky white of the bags, her skin would surely look like the finest of fine porcelain. "Your skin is as smooth and white as china," an old woman at the local public bath—a total stranger—had once told her. At the time Ginko was just a child, not even old enough to attend school. To her, china was something hard and cold that broke to smithereens when you dropped it. How she had hated that old woman and what she had said! Wouldn't she be pleased, though, if only someone would say that to her now.

When she turned on the television, it was in the middle of broadcasting news about a particularly grotesque murder. A body had been hacked into pieces and stuffed into garbage bags. The discovery had been made in an outlying suburb by a housewife who, when depositing her own garbage at the local collection site, couldn't help noticing some suspicious-looking bloody streaks inside one of the other see-through garbage bags. She went straight to the police. When they opened the bag, they found the severed remains of a human body. The rest of the corpse was scattered in dozens of garbage bags left at different collection sites throughout the neighborhood. The square-jawed announcer displayed no emotion as he read the news. His large mouth was the only moving part in an otherwise impassive face.

A moment ago Ginko had been ready to take off all her clothes, but she remembered that she wanted to go to the public bath. As she would have to get undressed there, she decided she might as well wait until then. There was no point in undressing twice. She was gradually returning to her normal state of mind, she felt, and it had made her want to watch television. After removing the upper bag that had been covering her head but with her legs still inside the bottom bag, she had hopped over to pick up the remote control. The instant she switched on the television, she saw them— her garbage bags—featured in the grisly murder.

The stack of garbage bags on the screen looked for all the world identical to the kind that Ginko always purchased. At her pharmacy this particular brand was the best buy, often costing two to three times less than other sizes and types. Why should she pay more for something she was going to throw out, Ginko reasoned. She wondered how much the killer had paid for the garbage bags he used. Were they already in the house or had he bought them expressly for the murder? Before the killing or afterwards? The price could have varied considerably. In light of the crime, it was an absurd thing to think about, but Ginko couldn't help herself. For no reason except that it was what she herself would have done, she decided that the killer had bought the cheapest bags available.

Ginko kept her eyes glued to the television screen as she waited impatiently for a glimpse of the bag containing the body parts. The camera panned to a shot of the roadside pickup site where garbage was piled in a heap. Having missed the first part of the broadcast, Ginko didn't know which suburb this was. There were garbage bags of all shapes and colors—clearly not everyone in this district was using the official bags. Which one held the human remains? She wanted to know. The announcer said nothing, and there were no captions on the screen. Of course the footage could just as easily have been shot after the police had taken away the evidence. It made her think about what had happened to the rest of the garbage, the real garbage. Had it been collected as usual? Or had all the garbage become part of the investigation, requiring the police to identify the contents of each bag and which household it came from? Had the new semi-transparent bags made their job any easier?

At the end of last year, a doctor had strangled his family and tried to dispose of their bodies in garbage bags. No mutilation that time—each family member was stuffed intact in a separate bag and thrown into the sea. The murderer was a young graduate of a prestigious medical school, and the victims were his wife and two small children. Again, the garbage bags he used were the white semi-transparent bags officially approved by the City. He said that he had simply used what he found at home, the bags purchased earlier by his wife. Could it have ever crossed her mind that she might one day find herself inside one of them?

Before the introduction of the new regulations, it wasn't totally unthinkable to use garbage bags to dispose of a cadaver.

"Jumbo" black vinyl garbage bags used to be a common sight everywhere, including at Ginko's apartment building. People liked the fact that no one could see what they were throwing out. Not only was the black vinyl completely opaque, the jumbo-size was much larger than the current twelve-gallon variety. A dead body inside one of those bags would probably have gone undetected. But before garbage began to be collected in plastic bags, what murderer in his right mind would have thought to put the body out on garbage day? Who ever heard of a corpse stuffed in a trash can? No, back then dead bodies were sealed in cardboard boxes or wrapped up in sheets, dumped deep in the mountains or concealed under floorboards.

The most original disposal method Ginko had ever heard of was the killer who attempted to get rid of his victim's body by boiling it in a tub. He used his own gas-heated bath and sealed up the windows and doorway from the inside with weather stripping so no telltale odor would escape. Day and night, he kept the water boiling hot. He thought he had pulled off the perfect crime, and would have too, had it not been for a suspicious meter reader who noticed that gas consumption for that month had jumped through the roof. By the time the police came calling, the corpse had disintegrated almost down to the bare bones.

Murder is a lot of work, Ginko thought to herself as she watched television. Too much for me. Not that Ginko need worry—she didn't have the nerve to commit murder. She was more likely to be killed than to do the killing.

At that moment the shadowy figure of the man in the stairwell flitted darkly across an inner corner of her mind, followed by another even less distinct shadow. Ginko's entire body shivered. Yes, how easy to be a murder victim. One minute you'd be caught off-guard daydreaming, the next instant you'd be dead. Ginko felt there was no guarantee she would never be killed. Wasn't it only a matter of luck that she hadn't been murdered by her own husband? When they'd been together, never once had she thought to be afraid of him, but then again, never once had she imagined how things would turn out.

At first Ginko had been at a total loss to comprehend what made a man like her husband tick. How could he have done what he did? Afterwards she became convinced that he'd planned everything from the start. If someone told her that her husband was a serial killer who chopped his victims into bits, she wouldn't have been surprised in the least.

To put an end to this line of thought, Ginko forced her attention back to the television screen. What on earth had the killer been thinking when he dumped the pieces of his murder victim just as they were into those see-through garbage bags? If people had garbage they didn't want others to see, the City advised wrapping it in paper or cloth before putting it in the bags. The killer should have heeded the City's instructions and wrapped up his "garbage" more carefully. Then he might have escaped detection.

Years ago, "garbage bag murders" were so sensational they always caused quite a stir, but no longer. After all, chopping up the body wasn't necessarily the killer's main aim. It was a disposal problem. Stuck for a way to get rid of the body, one solution was to carve up the remains and put them out with the garbage.

Of course, that was it! Ginko agreed with herself aloud, turning to examine her own body inside the garbage bag. You couldn't stuff a hundred-pound corpse into a twelve-gallon bag. Not only would it not fit, it would be way too heavy. As soon as the garbage collector picked it up, either the bag would burst or he would throw out his back.

Ginko knew exactly what she would do: first cut up the body, freeze all the parts and then dole them out in the garbage gradually one small piece at a time. In the future maybe people wouldn't be cremated in wooden coffins—they'd be zipped in calcium carbonate bags. Better for the crematorium furnace, better for the environment. But when her own time came, Ginko wondered, who would put her in a calcium carbonate bag? Not a single face came to mind. The ticklish sensation in her head was probably caused by her silly thoughts, but now everything was getting fuzzier and fuzzier. Suddenly her concentration snapped like a broken thread, and her mind went completely blank. Ginko gazed vacantly at the television set. The extra strong dose of painkillers she had taken earlier was starting to work, but Ginko had completely forgotten about taking them, forgotten even that she'd had a headache. All of a sudden she felt so weak and drained that even squatting in the bag required too much effort. She slowly rolled onto her side and shut her eyes. How good it felt! The bag was such an intimate part of her, it seemed like she had been living inside it for a very long time.

Although the upper bag she had thrown off in the kitchen earlier still retained the puffed-up shape of her form, it was slowly collapsing as the air inside escaped. Watching it was like looking at her own cast-off skin. She would get inside it again later, she thought dreamily, drifting off into a light sleep. When she woke, a program about hot springs was on television, reminding her about going to the public bath. She wanted to soak in a warm, brightly lit bath surrounded by other people. Once her mind was made up, her body seemed to move of its own accord, leaping nimbly out of the bag. Sometimes she found her own actions and thoughts as incomprehensible as a complete stranger's. She felt as if another woman, someone she didn't know, secretly shared her body and made her afraid of her own thoughts. That woman. A woman lacking in all sensitivity, someone cunning and deceitful. To Ginko, she was the woman her husband had brought and left behind.

Ginko crept silently down the back staircase one step at a time, holding her breath. What if the man she had encountered earlier was hiding somewhere? She tried to control her breathing as she checked for telltale signs, but fear was making her pant. She should have gone out the front entrance but she'd come down the back staircase out of habit without thinking and now it was too late. The real Ginko was a bit of a coward—cautious and overly earnest in all she did. That other woman, however, was completely indifferent to danger. She was coarse, the things she did slapdash and slipshod.

Originally it had never been her custom to take the back staircase. It was her husband who had liked to use it. Still, there was no denying the convenience—the back staircase was closer to her apartment—and so over time she came to use it regularly, even now despite her dislike.

Less than half a year after they married, Ginko's husband had disappeared without a word. That was six years ago. Precisely one half of the savings in her bank account also vanished with him. Fortunately the condominium was solely in her name as she had bought it when she was single—at least he wasn't able to run off with the ownership papers. She continued to pay her mortgage little by little from her monthly paycheck just as she had done all along before she had married.

Exactly where she had first met her husband Ginko couldn't really remember. He just seemed to have appeared at her side one day and just as casually they began seeing each other. Time passed and they drifted into marriage, a thoroughly pedestrian married life. With both of them working, there really wasn't much time to spend together. But they never argued—nothing had struck her as particularly odd. Except that there were moments when she felt truly mystified by what had prompted her to marry him. Never once had she felt overwhelmed by desire for this man. Perhaps it was that other woman inside her who had lured her into marriage, for the real Ginko tended to slide through life giving herself up to whatever happened. When her husband left and she returned to being alone, there was a part of her that experienced relief. Marriage had been unnatural; at some level she had always been aware that she felt no genuine interest in her husband. After he left, she was forced to face the fact that she hadn't known anything about him at all.

Before their marriage, Ginko's husband had lived in the bachelor housing provided by the company he worked for. One day he simply moved into Ginko's place and began commuting to work from there. Shortly afterwards they got married. Later Ginko discovered that much of what he had told her were lies: indeed, when she went to look for his company, she found it didn't exist. She even wondered whether the marriage itself was a fraud but a check of the City Hall records confirmed its legality. In fact, on paper she was still married.

There was no substantial change to her life. Just as before her marriage, she commuted to work everyday. When she came home, she did her housework, ate, and went to sleep. Monotonous maybe, but Ginko was not bored. A man had entered her life, then left, and the only change had been her surname. There were lots of women like her at the government office, women who got married and then suddenly went back to being single again. Look at her male colleagues, too—some were divorced, others were confirmed bachelors. In this day and age no one really cared. Except for having to put up with the occasional sarcastic innuendo from her boss, it was no big deal.

The problem if anything lay in the marriage system itself. At work Ginko was required to stamp official government documents with her seal, a seal carved with the characters for her husband's last name, the name of a swindler and thief. It struck her now as a suspiciously fake name. Each time she pressed the seal on a fresh document, though, she felt the thrill of being an accomplice in crime. From time to time, she worried about whether she was the wife of a bona fide criminal, but no one had ever said anything and she, too, kept her mouth shut.

Was his taking only half of her money meant as a gesture to their being a couple? That was the part that worried her. What if she died first and he came bounding back out of nowhere to file the inheritance papers and lay claim to the remaining half of the money, not to mention her condominium? Well, if that also meant he would see to her burial, so be it, she thought.

Looking back after the passage of six years, it struck Ginko that none of what had happened mattered very much. She was proud of herself for being able to take it all in stride. Yet if even someone as timid as Ginko could come to feel this way, how much less significance did everything that happened have in the mind of someone like her husband.

When she walked down the back staircase, she could almost hear her husband snickering from somewhere at the end of a closed sloping tunnel, laughing at the stupid wife he had managed to dupe. "What are you running from!" Ginko wanted to laugh right back as his footsteps hastened away. Very occasionally she recalled the touch of his embrace.

Whenever she went through this passageway and thought of her husband, Ginko was overcome by a bizarre sensation that beneath her meek exterior she herself was a wicked person. Yet once she opened the door and stepped outside, this feeling evaporated completely as if there were something unnatural about the air that hung stagnant in the back stairwell, something that drew out the evil hidden in the depths of every human heart.

Fires had broken out here by the back entrance, the first time five years ago and then again two years later. Although the fires had not been especially big, they'd left a scorched smell that lingered for some time, and for a while just walking through the area could make one's eyes sting. One of the apartment residents, a recyling enthusiast, had salvaged newspapers and magazines others had thrown away in the garbage and piled them in a corner behind the staircase. It was here that the fires had been set, both times at dawn. In neither case was the arsonist ever caught. Despite these incidents, no one complained when shortly over a year later a mountain of old newspapers began to form again in exactly the same spot. Even now there were stacks of newspapers and piles of thick comic books.

The arsonist surely couldn't have been her husband, and yet ... Ginko had no reason for having even this sliver of suspicion, only that her husband was the kind of man who was capable of doing anything, anything at all. But the fires had been set after his disappearance, so she did not feel too concerned.

The night a young woman was stabbed by the back door of the condominium, however, her husband was still living with her. Ginko had never found out if the attacker had been apprehended. What if ... ? Again, it was a very faint but persistent feeling of suspicion. Not that her husband had ever shown signs of such violence. No, the roots of Ginko's uncertainty lay in her own shock at realizing that she had lived for half a year with someone she didn't know at all.

The victim of the stabbing was the daughter of the sake shop owner. For several days after the incident the sake shop, which was located next to the public bath, remained closed, its metal shutters tightly fastened. When it reopened for business, it was as though nothing had happened, and an air of everyday ordinariness returned to the store. Not until over a month later did Ginko finally catch a glimpse of a young woman seated at the front of the store who she assumed must be the daughter. About twenty years old with dyed reddish-orange hair and a sullen, petulant expression, she had the look of a juvenile delinquent. She glared at passers-by with a mean unfriendly stare. Ginko herself had been at the receiving end of one of these looks and, flustered, had quickly averted her gaze.

There would have been no reason for her husband to attack a young woman like that. But not having a reason was no reason for not doing something, as Ginko herself knew only too well. After all there had been no pressing reason for her to marry her husband and yet she had. Perhaps her husband had not really intended to swindle her from the outset, but only later, for no reason at all, was simply struck by the urge.

Either way it didn't matter. Ginko no longer cared if her husband had been the attacker or not.

When the stabbing incident took place, her husband had been out of the apartment. Already fast asleep, Ginko hadn't noticed his departure. She woke at the sound of his return.

"What happened?" she asked.

When he heard her voice in the pitch dark, he turned on the light in the entranceway. Although he had been lying in bed beside her just a short while ago, now he was wearing a loose jacket over his pajamas.

"Nothing," he replied, but he sounded slightly short of breath. Cold air seemed to flow from his body.

"You went outside, didn't you?" she said.

"No, not really."

"Then what are you doing wearing that outfit in the middle of the night?"

It wasn't unusual for her husband to be up by himself till very late at night. Ginko, who couldn't function the next day without enough rest, was always sound asleep before midnight. Generally she slept straight through to morning and had no idea what time her husband finally came to bed. In the mornings they would rise together, have a rushed breakfast, and Ginko would leave the house first. From the time they had begun living together, they had always led separate lives—astonishingly little time had been spent getting to know each other. All in all, it was not a very good marriage.

"Forget it. Let's go to sleep."

"Go to sleep ... I was asleep till you woke me up." Ginko was grouchy at having been woken. It may also have been around this time that she was beginning to feel impatient with the relationship. Living together had no meaning.

"Sorry. I heard some noise outside so I went to take a look," her husband said.

"What was it?"

Her husband turned away as if tired of being pestered. At that instant the sound of an ambulance siren started up in the distance. It was followed by the whine of a police car siren, and the throbbing of the two sirens wove together in the night air as they drew closer and closer. Within seconds they were right outside the condominium engulfing it in a blaring sea of sound.

"So they're here at last," her husband murmured.

"There must have been a traffic accident," Ginko said quietly. She remembered clearly how she didn't believe it herself, not for a moment. Deep down she knew that there was some connection between the sirens outside and the way her husband had slipped back silently to their apartment. She felt suspicious yet she could not imagine what he might have done.

Her husband said nothing more. Throughout her long, sleepless night, the sirens continued to ring in her ears. From the rhythm of his breathing beside her, she knew her husband couldn't sleep either.

It wasn't until the following evening when she stopped by the local vegetable store on her way home from work that she found out what had happened. As soon as she saw Ginko, the greengrocer's wife drew her face up close and whispered, "That was at your apartment building last night, wasn't it? The sake store daughter was stabbed, they say. So shocking! Store's closed today, of course. They must all be over at the hospital."

Ginko listened in silence as the greengrocer's wife excitedly shared everything she knew. The sake shop was located diagonally across the street from the vegetable store.

"Have they caught the assailant?" she asked.

"Oh. ... I don't know." The greengrocer's wife suddenly lost her confident tone. "I haven't heard. Oh, they're bound to catch him quick. If not, well, that's pretty terrifying, isn't it?"

Ginko hurried back home, locked the door, and drew the chain. She rifled through the evening newspaper where the greengrocer's wife said the news had been reported. What she found was a very short article stating simply that a woman had been stabbed. There were no details: no mention of anyone from the sake shop and nothing about the attacker who was still at large. She rushed into the bedroom and pulled out her husband's pajamas and jacket. No blood, thank goodness. Although she didn't really believe her husband was the attacker, she still couldn't relax. Even if he hadn't done it, he was hiding something.

Waiting for her husband's return, her heart nearly stopped each time she heard footsteps in the hallway. Looking back afterwards, it seemed that even then her body had already detected her husband's impending betrayal of her. Or maybe it was her own suspicions that had driven him away.

When her husband finally came home that evening, Ginko told him about the stabbing and demanded to know what he had been doing outside the night before. It must have been clear she doubted him, but she was past caring what he thought.

For the longest time he simply glared at her, his mouth clamped tightly shut. She was afraid he might strike her. Not that he had ever hit her before, but she had never made him angry and had no idea how he would react, so much of a mystery was he to her.

"I thought I heard a scream," he said in a flat tone edged with anger. "If you hear a woman scream in the middle of the night, you can't just do nothing."

Ginko couldn't believe her own ears. Her husband? Was he really the type to ignore all personal danger and respond to a woman's cry for help in the middle of the night?

He had dashed out of the apartment immediately but returned to get something he could use as a weapon. He'd grabbed that hanging flower vase, he said, pointing to the empty tin hook in the entranceway where it normally hung.

"I didn't know what direction the scream had come from," he continued. "I was looking around trying to figure out which way to go, but by then other people had come out, so I thought it was okay and came home."

It could have been true. It could have been a bald lie. If he had used the back stairway, it was thirty seconds to the rear door.

Returning to the apartment and looking around for something like the flower vase to grab would have added another minute, maybe two at the most. If he'd gone out the front door of the building and run around to the back, another two to three minutes. By that time others might have gathered outside. Maybe. As a rule, though, no matter what has happened, apartment dwellers rarely open their doors in the middle of the night.

But her husband's story had some ring of truth. She could picture him hearing a scream, waiting until he finally heard other people outside, and then and only then venturing out himself.

When Ginko opened the back door of her building and stepped outside, she was amazed at how brilliantly the moon shone. The sky was filled with stars. She walked past the sake shop where the lights were still on. Ducking her head under the curtain that hung across the entranceway, she entered the public bathhouse.

Entry to both the men's and women's baths was through the same main doorway which opened into a large wooden-floored lobby where the clerk collected money. After paying, one proceeded through one of the doors flanking the clerk's desk into either the men's or women's bathing areas. It was quite different from the old-fashioned public bathhouse where the clerk was perched high above both baths and had a good view of everyone naked.

The bath was not very big, although it was probably no smaller than a typical old-fashioned public bath. It looked like there was less room because of the way it was divided into separate narrow tubs, each tub containing a different type of special bath water: one was filled with murky hot spring water, one had Jacuzzi jets, yet another had water that gave off an eerie reddish glow. Ginko wanted to soak in all of them but each of the five separate tubs was currently occupied. There was really only enough room for one person to fit comfortably—two were a bit of a squeeze, the tubs were that small.

While waiting for one of the tubs to become free, Ginko washed her body leisurely. She noticed that turnover was rapid. As soon as a second woman entered one of the tubs, it seemed the first occupant would feel obliged to leave.

Ten women of all ages sat washing themselves in a crowded line along the row of faucets. Most of the women appeared to have come alone. There were no children, no voices in conversation. The lack of chatter, in particular, lent an abnormal quiet to what should have been a lively bathhouse. The only sounds were the splashing of running water as someone washed her hair at the shower taps and the burping, percolating sound of water in the hot tubs. The wash buckets provided were plastic, not metal, so even the banging of buckets on the tile flooring was subdued. Two young women squatted closely side by side at neighboring wash faucets, but it was impossible to tell if they had come together or were complete strangers. Neither looked at the other as they washed their naked bodies in silence.

Ginko looked at the reflection of her now slackening body in the mirror and remembered how the day after she had slept with a man for the first time, she had come to the public bath and scrubbed and scrubbed her body. After only one night her body seemed to have been transformed into a different substance, had turned as soft as rubber. The woman sealed inside that thin, fine layer of white skin seemed so vulnerable and insubstantial. Even her nerves felt like they had been polished down to their very tips. Lost in thought she had absentmindedly rubbed her sponge over and over her body. She hadn't looked at the mirror in front of her once. She could feel her beauty and her youth through her fingertips, she didn't need the confirmation of a mirror. She had been twenty-four years old then.

The time her husband ran away, she had also come here to bathe. But her body had felt like an unfamiliar shape, and her hands had slipped awkwardly this way and that as she tried to wash. It had been a slow, tedious process. When the plastic washbasin she was holding slipped from her hands, she had heard a dry, high-pitched crackling that sliced right through the hot, moist air of the bathhouse. She had soaked for a long time in the tub filled with clear, glowing red water: it contained a special stone brought over from China that was supposed to release medicinal properties into the water when it was heated. Good for the nerves, the sign had said. It was indeed a very relaxing bath with a soft, murmuring babble. At one end of the tub there had been something resembling a heater enclosed in a steel cage. The stone inside glowed red, like at a sauna, and the reddish light spread through the bath water. Ginko's skin, too, had glowed with a beautiful pink luminosity.

She must have stayed in too long that time for she had suddenly felt faint and hastily pulled herself out of the tub. She had managed to stagger to the changing room but then, still stark naked, collapsed on the floor. The other women, also naked, all crowded around her. Are you alright, asked a young woman bringing her face down close to Ginko's. She was a slim woman but had an extremely voluptuous figure. As Ginko gazed up at her, she had felt an overwhelming desire to be sucked right inside that woman's body.

"I'm fine, really, I just got a bit dizzy," Ginko had assured her in a hoarse voice. The woman nodded and moved away. Just then from the men's side, a loud arrogant voice had boomed across the partition.

"Hey, where's my soap? There's no soap!"

"Isn't it there?" A woman's voice responded.

"No, it's not here," the man continued. "How come you didn't bring my soap!"

The woman had hung her head. "I guess I didn't bring it," she murmured in a voice no louder than a soft sigh, yet Ginko had heard her quite distinctly.

"How come you didn't bring my soap. How the hell am I supposed to wash without soap!"

The woman had made no attempt to reply. She simply stared hard at the partition between the men's and women's baths, her eyes sad and empty.

"How come there's no soap! Answer me!"

Seemingly oblivious to the other male customers around him, the man's voice had become a petulant whine. On their side, the naked women began to giggle. The woman, whose skin was like delicate porcelain, looked tired and embarrassed. Suddenly she had curled her lips, and letting an unmistakable smirk rise to her face, turned her back to the partition. Though the man's volley of complaints continued, she refused to face the direction of his words. Then, picking up her towel and her soap, she had sauntered casually into the bath.

The tub with the murky hot spring water was now free. Ginko got up, walked over, and sank in up to her neck. Against her skin the water felt slightly gritty as if it contained tiny particles of calcium carbonate. It was like being inside her garbage bag.

∾

Water

When Ikuri got home from the plant on Friday evening, there was a folded note marked "Urgent!" pinned to the door of her apartment. It sent her into a momentary state of confusion.

Just before leaving the factory, she'd sent a love letter to one of her co-workers. Was this a reply from him? Already? For a second Ikuri felt a violent throbbing in her breast. But it wasn't possible. The love letter had left her hands only forty-five minutes ago. Still, who else could it be from?

She'd enlisted the help of a girlfriend at work who slipped the letter into a thin business envelope to make it look like an office memo. At a little before five o'clock, the woman had called Ikuri at her work station confirming safe delivery of the missive. The object of all this attention was Aotsuka Akira, one of the mechanics in charge of maintaining the plant's heavy machinery and the type of guy who did his job with a "see-how-much-I-love-my-work" kind of enthusiasm.

Ikuri was confident she wasn't going to be rejected, but there were still lots of unknowns. How would the relationship get started? How would it progress? What would happen in the end? This much she did know—sometime between now and Monday evening, she could expect Akira at her apartment ringing her doorbell. She decided that Saturday and Sunday weren't very likely, so unless he came tonight, then Monday would be it. Yes, sometime during the day on Monday he would casually drop by her work area to check if she were really serious. But for the whole weekend, he wouldn't be able to get Ikuri off his mind.

You couldn't get a lover by being passive and mute. You had to do something, make a real effort, and Ikuri believed in working hard to achieve what she wanted. But she also knew that not everything was going to fall into her lap. She had no intention of being caught off guard by a rejection letter, not even one sent express mail.

Plucking the piece of paper from the door, Ikuri held it up to the overhead fluorescent light in the hallway. The note was not in an envelope but simply folded twice. She could make out some faint scribbling, but she had no idea what Akira's handwriting looked like. The word "Urgent!" had been scrawled in ink on the outside of the note in a crude, sloppy hand. Ikuri's own letter to Akira had been composed on a word processor and printed with a fresh ink cartridge. Thank goodness she hadn't sent something handwritten.

It was so confusing! While she hoped this was a reply from Akira, at the same time she hoped it wasn't. No matter how unlikely it was to be from him, it wasn't entirely outside the realm of possibility. In her letter Ikuri had included a detailed map with directions from the plant to her apartment building, even specifying travel time. If Akira had bolted out of the factory the instant work ended and raced over by car, he could easily have beaten her home. Possible, yes, but Ikuri's instinct told her otherwise. No, at this very moment Akira was probably reading and re-reading her letter. For the umpteenth time.

Indeed, the note was not from Akira. It was from the building superintendent. In a cramped, hard to read scrawl, the note said that the occupant of the apartment directly below Ikuri, a certain Mr. Takayama, had complained about water leaking from his ceiling and could Ikuri please contact the superintendent as soon as she got home. At the bottom was the date and time of writing. The note must have been pinned to her door around ten o'clock this morning.

Ikuri checked her watch: 5:45 P.M. The superintendent, who only worked between 8:30 and 3:30, was already gone for the day. Passing his office on her way in, Ikuri had noticed the closed sign and the white curtain drawn across the reception window—she couldn't get in touch with him even if she wanted to. For people with regular jobs, contacting the superintendent was virtually impossible.

Of all days for this to happen, Ikuri thought as she hurriedly unlocked the door to her apartment. Too impatient even to turn on the light, she gave her place a quick inspection in the semi-darkness. Nothing appeared out of the ordinary.

She flipped the light switch. She hadn't had enough sleep the night before, and the bright fluorescent light hurt like needles in her eyes. The room, now fully lit, again showed absolutely no signs of abnormality.

Last night after composing her letter to Akira and in anticipation of his possible visit today, Ikuri had assiduously cleaned her apartment with even more care than usual. It was a tiny one-room studio, quick to get messy but a snap to tidy up.

Crouching in the lowered entryway with her shoes still on, Ikuri bent forward and rubbed her hand across the carpeted floor. The only dampness she felt was from the sweat on her own palms, caused by carrying the heavy bags of groceries she'd bought in the local store on her way home.

Ikuri next spread several sheets of tissue paper on the carpet and pressed them flat with the palm of her hand, experimenting in a number of different spots. The white tissues remained bone dry.

They picked up the odd bit of fluff that her vacuum cleaner had missed but there was not a trace of moisture. Then she stepped onto the carpet in her bare feet, and concentrating hard on what she felt on her soles, walked slowly all the way over to the kitchen sink.

She breathed a sigh of relief. The floor was bone dry, conclusively. The water faucet was tightly shut—there wasn't even a drop of water in the sink basin. The toilet and bathtub were also fine. If anything, the room felt too dry. Ikuri opened the window and let the darkening air rush in.

This unexpected task had thrown her off kilter. She decided not to bother with any dinner preparations as the likelihood of Akira showing up tonight was quite low. On her own Ikuri hardly ever bothered with dinner as she found that eating a hearty lunch in the subsidized factory dining hall tided her right through the evening.

Once again she took in the details of her little nest. It was not a bad lifestyle. She worked where she liked, lived where she liked, invited whatever men she liked back to her place. Almost thirty, she felt she'd finally hit her stride.

She had managed to get the down payment for the condominium from her parents. It was her little castle. Although not brand new—the building was already about twelve years old—the condo was hers, and when she was at home Ikuri felt safe, self-confident, happy. Yes, one's living space was crucial!

Until as recently as eleven months ago, she had been a tenant in a thirty-year-old building whose main redeeming feature was the cheap rent. No matter how lightly she tread, the tatami mats squeaked, and a strong wind could make the entire apartment rattle as air whistled through its corners. Living there, Ikuri couldn't help but feel she was a miserable, inadequate human being.

Something as simple as moving to a new place had brought her such bliss. Oh, she was very grateful for the money and, of course, to her parents who had been the source of her funding.

She gazed around her apartment dreamily. If only Akira could see it, how impressed he'd be. Anyone who realized that Ikuri actually owned all of this was bound to be filled with envy.

The closets and drawers in the apartment were built-in so the only large piece of furniture Ikuri owned was a Western-style bed. Instead of a dining table, she ate off an old-fashioned Japanese-style writing desk which had belonged to her father in his bachelor days. When her parents got divorced, her mother had kept it hidden in the back of a closet, never bothering to return it. When her mother later remarried, Ikuri took the opportunity to claim the desk as hers. It was just an ordinary old thing, but she was attached to it. She didn't need other tables or chairs.

Ikuri strained hard, trying to catch signs of life in the apartment downstairs. Nothing. She even went out onto the balcony and tried peering below. At least for the time being, there didn't seem to be anyone home. No one who might be inclined to yell and scream at her.

Didn't a leak in the apartment downstairs mean the same thing could happen in her apartment? This possibility had never once crossed her mind before. Ikuri plunked herself down in the middle of the floor and surveyed her room again. She was always very careful when it came to water and gas. She emptied her bath water every night rather than save it in the tub as some people did for use the next evening. Before going out, she never failed to turn off the gas. Her parents had cautioned her that it only took one slip to cause a disaster.

Ikuri had never met her downstairs neighbor and had no idea what he looked like. But, after all, she hadn't been living here very long and she was out all day at work. For that matter, she could barely remember the superintendent's face. The only image she retained was of a skinny, nervous-looking man about sixty years old. As Ikuri left for work every morning at eight and returned in the evening around six, her only opportunity for seeing the superintendent was on Saturdays.

After some consideration, Ikuri decided there was really no need for her to go out of her way to talk to her downstairs neighbor. A letter to the superintendent would do. Anyway, he'd written her a note, so she'd write him back. When it came to composing letters, Ikuri was not without a certain amount of confidence. This was how she had persuaded her parents to give her the down payment for her condo. Just one letter written separately to each parent, and in no time substantial funds had been transferred into her bank account.

> *Dear _____,*
>
> *I have received and read your letter. About the matter of a leak in the premises below mine, there is absolutely no question of any water being spilled in my apartment. I am writing to assure you of this.*
>
> *Sincerely, _____*

Ikuri signed the letter and appended the date and time. She did not enclose it in an envelope but simply folded it twice. Going downstairs to the mailroom on the first floor, she dropped it into the superintendent's box located at the far end of the residents' mailboxes. At the same time she confirmed that the name on the mailbox for apartment 304 was indeed "Mr. Takayama." His box was empty.

Although she'd never met the owner of 304, Ikuri knew the apartment, for she had once mistaken it for her own. Preoccupied at the time, she hadn't even noticed the nameplate and had stuck her key in the lock. She'd taken the stairs that time, and wasn't paying attention to what floor she was on. When she took the elevator, she pushed the button for her floor, so there was no room for this kind of error, but taking the stairs was another matter. On another occasion she'd made the same mistake with the apartment upstairs. Each time she'd been so bewildered why her door wouldn't open that she'd rattled the knob desperately for some time. She was only lucky that no one had been in.

How could she possibly settle down! Even if she had decided in her own mind that Akira was not coming tonight, her body remained in a state of anxious anticipation and her ears pricked up at the slightest sound beyond the apartment door. Her imagination raced to fantasies of the changes in her life that lay around the corner. But what if Akira didn't come at all? Just picturing that awkward moment when the two of them met at the factory both thrilled and exhausted her.

It wasn't until after eleven o'clock that, with great relief, she was able to reclaim time for herself. She quietly took a shower and got ready for bed. Then she washed some grapes for tomorrow's breakfast, cradling them under the faucet with both hands. They were a special variety, slightly flat on the sides, sent by her mother who ran a vineyard. As soon as the running water made contact with the grapes, though, it sprayed upwards in a fountain. Panicking, Ikuri quickly shut off the tap. Fortunately hardly any water had splashed outside the sink. She plucked off several grapes and stuffed them in her mouth all at once, savoring the mix of sweet and acidic juices.

Suddenly she was struck by the urge to compose a letter to someone, anyone. But she had just written one to Akira and to follow so soon with another might make her look a bit nutty.

Whenever Ikuri was interested in a man, she sent a love letter. She simply had to do it—she couldn't help herself. Success wasn't guaranteed, of course, but knowing that the recipient of the letter was intrigued, even if only temporarily, gave her a profound sense of satisfaction. Trying to communicate through conversation or behavior was tedious and clumsy. Not only did it take a lot of time, Ikuri did not think her feelings came across very accurately.

She felt no particular need for friends. Her goal was to meet as many men as possible, not because she craved popularity but because it increased her chances of meeting Mr. Right. Her attitude about work was the same. Since her first short stint as a high school chemistry teacher, she had job-hopped constantly—cram school instructor, office lady at an advertising firm, bookstore employee, bakery worker, receptionist at a shipping company. Currently she worked on the assembly line at a plant that manufactured clocks. Her co-workers thought she was weird. Why would a college grad want to work in a factory? But Ikuri was sure she wasn't the only blue-collar worker with a university degree and, besides, she was well suited to work that required manual dexterity. Of course, it wasn't perfect. There would be something else later, something to which she was even better suited. When she got bored with her present job, she was planning to get a small truck and try her hand at delivery work, picking up subcontracts.

Right now, though, her future was out of focus. After all, she didn't yet know—couldn't even imagine—what kind of lover or husband would enter her life. Maybe Aotsuka Akira was the one, maybe not. Of course, she might remain single forever, and if she knew that in advance it would certainly make planning her life easier. As it was, however, she felt as if things were on hold, a depressing situation for someone almost thirty years old. At the thought of meeting someone special and getting married, though, Ikuri's chest inexplicably tightened with excitement.

"That man, he's looking at you again."

The kindly older woman who worked in the plant's business office had recently befriended Ikuri and taken it upon herself to bring Akira to her attention.

"He's a catch. If you can snag him, he'll make you happy. Call it my sixth sense, but I'm never wrong."

The woman was married and constantly recommended the state of matrimony to Ikuri. Meanwhile, Ikuri couldn't decide if the woman was madly in love with her husband or bored out of her mind.

Actually, Ikuri had secretly had her eye on Akira long before he began noticing her. She used to fix her gaze on his back, staring at him for as long as she could as if to penetrate deep into his very body. Ikuri was convinced that her gaze had saturated Akira to the point of overflow and that now it was brimming over and streaming back to her.

It had taken about four months from the time when Ikuri first began looking at Akira to the time when he began noticing her. Any man who came around after just a glance or two was no good and probably did not have much going for him. This was a serious business, after all. Ikuri's instinct told her that Akira was definitely marriage material. It was important to trust one's instincts, especially if they suited your convenience.

Years ago when she was a teacher, a colleague had misinterpreted a casual encounter they'd had and persisted in forcing his affections on her. More than ten years her senior, with a wife and children, he was the one who stood to suffer if word got around, yet he would boast about their relationship in front of others in the apparent belief that this was how to chalk up his achievements as a lover.

After Ikuri broke up with him, the man fell into a deep depression and began spinning his own account of tragic love. When Ikuri refused to continue the relationship, he turned bitter. "You think you can use me as much as you want and then just throw me away. I risked everything I have for you, but women like you only know how to toy with men." It was so idiotic Ikuri couldn't even be bothered protesting.

Who wanted something useless shoved in your face? What you don't need, dump! That was just the way things were. But if there was something you really wanted, Ikuri thought, you should do everything in your power to obtain it, and once you've got it, better hang on tight!

When the telephone rang Saturday morning Ikuri was still asleep. She woke with a start, and her first thought was it must be Akira calling to reject her. Then she remembered that she hadn't given him her telephone number. Relieved, she picked up the receiver.

"Hello, it's the building superintendent. I left a note on your door yesterday. I wonder if you've had a chance to read it."

"Yes."

"The man living below you, Mr. Takayama, says water is leaking from his ceiling. I wonder if you might have spilled any water?" The superintendent was simply repeating by phone what he'd written in his note. Ikuri stifled a yawn.

"Yes, that's what you said in your note. I wrote you a reply and put it in your mailbox."

"Yes, I got it."

"Well, it should be clear from my note. I haven't spilled any water."

"Oh, I see ... but I've just had a call from Mr. Takayama again and he says that the leaking hasn't stopped. He was very threatening. Are you sure you can't do anything?"

"You're making this rather difficult." Ikuri's head was still woolly with sleep, and she was having a hard time making out the superintendent's voice which seemed to echo along the telephone line as if it were traveling a long distance. What a dense man! Nonetheless Ikuri couldn't help looking up at her own ceiling anxiously for leaks, then quickly realizing her mistake, shifted her gaze to the floor. Tugging on the telephone cord, she crouched low and with her free hand rubbed the surface of the carpet. Definitely dry as a bone.

"I'm afraid there's no water here. I can't help you. You'll have to look somewhere else."

"Oh, I see ... uhhh, yes, look somewhere else. But where? I really don't know. I'm afraid it's quite beyond me. Meanwhile Mr. Takayama is furious! I would call the maintenance company but they're closed today and there's no way of getting in touch. I should have called them yesterday, but yesterday you weren't in and contacting you first seemed to make the most sense. Anyway, I'm not a plumber. It wouldn't do for someone like me to be fiddling with things." The superintendent spoke in a flat monotone, almost as if talking about someone else's problem.

"Well, as I've indicated, this has nothing to do with me," Ikuri said.

"Oh, I see ..."

"Oh, I see" seemed to be his favorite expression. As Ikuri's head cleared of sleep, she found herself becoming increasingly enraged. She was tempted to hang up, but the superintendent was relentlessly droning on and on.

"I just came from Mr. Takayama's apartment. There's a

stain on the ceiling running from the front doorway all the way to the kitchen sink, and every so often water drips down. I was wondering if Mr. Takayama and I could pay you a short visit and look around your place. If Mr. Takayama could see for himself that nothing is leaking there, then I'm sure he'll be more disposed to the idea of investigating other avenues."

So that was it. Ikuri could now see what was going on. Mr. what's-his-face Takayama had already decided that she was at fault.

"I don't appreciate being accused of something I haven't done. Okay, you can inspect my apartment, but I don't think it will be necessary to bring Mr. Takayama. You're the super. You can come alone and then report your findings to him. I'll get changed and tidy up. Could you come in an hour?"

"I really think it would be better if Mr. Takayama could take a look himself. I'm caught in the middle here. Really, I have no authority ..."

"Excuse me," Ikuri interrupted, "are you suggesting that I let a man—a total stranger—come into my apartment? No way! I'm a woman living alone."

"Oh, I see ..."

"Good!" Ikuri slammed the telephone receiver. This was no joking matter. What was wrong with that man!

Now her whole morning was spoiled. But she felt a bit of satisfaction knowing that at least she had managed to turn down Takayama's demand. Of course, her apartment was spotless, there was no need for cleaning up. Ikuri hurriedly got dressed and, as a precaution, inspected the entire premises once again for signs of water leakage. What had happened in the apartment downstairs, she wondered. It was one thing if she had carelessly spilled water on the floor, but when a leak sprang with no apparent cause ... well, it probably wouldn't be easy to solve.

An hour later the superintendent appeared. Alone, as instructed.

"Sorry to bother you on your day off," he began. "Well, what's the situation here?"

"Situation? There is no 'situation.' I told you there's nothing to see but you insisted on inspecting. So go ahead. Look around to your heart's content."

Ikuri showed the superintendent everything there was to see— the toilet, the bathtub, the washing machine, the kitchen sink, the humidifier she kept by the side of the entryway, the main water pipe. It was such a tiny apartment there was scarcely any need for a guided tour, but without it the superintendent gave no sign of making a move on his own. Wherever Ikuri pointed he perfunctorily tested for dampness with his fingers. They repeated the routine around the apartment. There was no sign of a leak anywhere, he readily acknowledged.

"Well, it's a mystery. Why should there be a leak downstairs if there's no water here? Maybe there's a hole in one of the pipes. Sometimes they rust right through, don't they? And this building isn't exactly new. Oh well, it'll just have to wait for a proper maintenance man. With something like this, a rank amateur like me can't tell up from down." After tossing off these irresponsible remarks, the superintendent smiled sheepishly.

"Everything's closed today and tomorrow. I'll call the head office Monday morning and have them send a repairman," he continued.

"Don't bother telling me. Tell that to the person downstairs," said Ikuri.

"On the surface, places like this look like they're built for convenience. Inside though, you never know what's what. I don't live here so I really can't say, but it seems to me that it's not convenient at all."

His official business over, the superintendent had suddenly become very familiar and, despite his taciturn appearance, surprisingly garrulous.

"What kind of person is the man downstairs, Mr. Takayama?" Ikuri asked.

"You don't know him?"

"No, I've never met him."

"Yup, that's what it's like in places like this."

"Well, there's never been any need to meet."

"I haven't been here that long myself," the superintendent said. "Can't say I've met everyone either. Okay, leave it up to me. I'll contact Mr. Takayama and tell him whatever."

"Wait a minute. Telling him 'whatever' is not good enough. I have nothing to do with his problem and I want you to make that perfectly clear." Ikuri studied the expression on the superintendent's face as she spoke.

"Oh, I see ... I didn't mean to ..."

Judging by the superintendent's reaction, Ikuri concluded that the man downstairs was not a very pleasant person and that she was lucky not to have been yelled at so far. Yes, it was just as well that Akira hadn't come last night.

The whole day was going to the dogs. Thirty minutes after leaving Ikuri's apartment, the superintendent called again to report that Mr. Takayama would not be satisfied until he saw the inside of Ikuri's apartment with his own eyes.

"Let me turn over the phone," continued the superintendent. "Can you please talk to him."

Before Ikuri had a chance to reply, a different voice came on the line.

"Why the hell won't you let me see your apartment! My

ceiling's been leaking since yesterday. Do you have any idea what I've been going through? It's only natural I'd want to see the apartment above me. I find it pretty strange that you don't want anyone seeing your place. What are you hiding? What do you think I'm going to do, tear your place apart? All I want is to see it with my own eyes, then I'll be satisfied."

What a loud, bellowing voice he had! Not to be cowed, Ikuri replied in a voice every bit as loud.

"That's precisely why I had the super come in and inspect. He can confirm there's nothing wrong. Why that is not good enough for you is beyond me."

From the other end of the line came a snorting guffaw.

"All I want is one quick look with my own eyes and I'll be satisfied. I don't get you at all."

"I would like to speak to the superintendent again. Please put him back on the line."

Ikuri did her best to speak in a neutral tone that betrayed no emotion. The only way to deal with such belligerence and downright rudeness was with icy formality.

"Very well, one visit," she said to the superintendent when he came on the phone. "But you will have to accompany him."

After the superintendent agreed, Ikuri hung up. She wanted to cry. Akira was supposed to be the first man to come to her new apartment, not this parade of intruders.

The two men were at her door within minutes. The first to enter was the superintendent, wearing a hangdog expression. Behind him was an overweight, middle-aged man in a black cardigan who pushed his way inside without so much as an "excuse me" or "hello." He had an unclean look to him, his cheeks darkened with stubble. He ogled everything in the apartment without the least bit of shame, but studiously ignored Ikuri, refusing to make eye contact or acknowledge her in any way.

"Sorry to bother you again on your holiday," began the superintendent bowing his head, "but this is very important to Mr. Takayama."

"Some 'holiday' I'm having!" Takayama muttered under his breath.

Ikuri decided to ignore him. She left everything up to the superintendent, standing back and observing from the distance. She was conscious of Takayama's dirty sandals, a glaring eyesore left in her entranceway. The man himself was a walking solid block of suspicion. He made no attempt to mask the ill-temper plainly evident in his piercing glare. But search as much as he liked, there was no finding something that didn't exist. After exhausting every possibility, the two men finally looked at each other wearily.

"Well?" Ikuri waited for the right moment to address the superintendent.

"Like when I was here earlier, I can't see any sign of a leak. The water must be coming from somewhere else and flowed in a funny direction till unfortunately it ended up over Mr. Takayama's ceiling. That's how I see it. It's right here, isn't it? Isn't this the spot where the water is leaking?"

"But as you can see, there is absolutely nothing on my floor." Ikuri repeated what she had said so many times earlier. Standing next to the superintendent, Takayama groaned.

"Water's leaking. That's a fact." Takayama turned his face away, his lips contorted in pain. Seeing Ikuri's apartment should have convinced him, but he didn't seem able or willing to accept the facts in front of his own eyes. Why had he bothered to come, she wanted to ask. When the superintendent suggested that it was time for them to leave, Takayama cast a mournful look back over the apartment as if reluctant to go.

His body was halfway out the door when he suddenly turned around and spoke to Ikuri for the first time. "Come with me, why don't you. Take a look at my ceiling. You don't like me, but if you saw my place you'd understand how I feel."

Ikuri curtly declined and, stone-faced, watched him leave.

As soon as the two men left, Ikuri felt that the value of her apartment had plummeted. Disheartened and depressed, she wished she could slosh water all over the room and scrub it thoroughly from top to bottom. Takayama made her feel sick to her stomach. Out of spite, she stomped furiously on the floor. To think that she was living above the lowest specimen of human being! So what if he hated her!

Ikuri wondered if she could hear anything from the apartment below. She concentrated hard but it seemed that all she could hear was the hum of silence expanding inside her own ears. Yet by remaining perfectly still, she soon discovered that indeed she was able to make out very faint sounds coming from different directions. She got down on her stomach and pressed her ear flat against the floor. Much to her surprise, she could hear people talking as clearly as if they were standing right next to her. Packets of sound and voices from faraway were traveling directly in her direction. She heard the sound of running water like several rivers coursing through her head. She heard the television, music, the sound of someone crying. But it was impossible to tell where the sounds were coming from. In fact, it felt as if the sounds originated from deep inside her own body. She slept in her Western-style bed high off the floor, so except for the traffic outside, she had never heard anything, not even a peep from the floor above her. She had been so confident of how solid and safe her "castle" was.

Listening became an obsession. The more she practiced, the more sounds she could hear, the greater her skill in distinguishing one from the other. She even thought she could hear the sound of dripping water. If she concentrated solely on that sound and blocked out all the other noise, sure enough every few seconds at regular intervals, there would be a soft drip. She imagined the light spray of water as it hit the floor. Before she knew it, she became incapable of not hearing the water.

Now she couldn't stop. She spent the entire weekend lying flat on her stomach on the floor, listening for sounds. The ringing of the telephone downstairs was particularly clear, and she could hear a man, presumably Takayama, chattering talkatively. It sounded like he was complaining about this or that, but Ikuri couldn't make out the content. It was definitely a male voice but whether it was Takayama or not she didn't know for sure.

When she closed her eyes and concentrated on listening, she felt as if she were floating in space on a thin plank of floor. Just beyond the walls of her apartment, there were others like her, also floating in midair. Above and below, to her left and right, in sealed capsules of space, solitary soulless individuals defending their own territory. How tempting to drill a small opening in the floor and pour water down, or to punch little holes in the walls and spray water through like a shower. She would love to see the reaction on everyone's face.

Ikuri's building was a tall, narrow twelve-story structure designed for bachelor condominums. On each floor, there were eight apartments, four on each side. She pictured her building as a clear glass box: twelve layers, eight compartments each. She would insert a bug shaped like a human being into every compartment, alternating male and female. She held her breath, feeling that she too was one of those bugs. Rolling onto her back, she slowly spread her arms and legs, quietly breathing in and out. You're in a glass room, she told herself. Watch out, everyone can see you. She sensed that all eyes in the building were staring at her body.

During the afternoon break on Monday, Ikuri and her friend, the older woman in the business office, sat on the lawn outside the factory basking in the hot rays of the sun. After a weekend spent cooped up inside, Ikuri wished she could run across the grass and soar unconstrained through the vast blue sky."There are underground springs in this area." Her friend was explaining why the ground they were sitting on was so damp. "That's the reason they originally built factories here in the first place. Even now if you dig down, you'll hit water."

Sure, water was okay as long as it came in the form of rain or an underground spring, but let a few drops fall from someone's ceiling and there was a big uproar. In the warm embrace of the sun's rays, though, anyone would feel good. That man downstairs, Takayama, should try relaxing outside a bit.

In the distance the figure of a young man clad in white mechanic's overalls was making his way towards Ikuri, moving as stiffly as if he were walking in outer space. Ikuri's friend gave her a nudge in the ribs with her elbow. "I'll go back ahead of you," she announced and lightly sprang off. Akira brushed past her as he continued his approach.

He barely stopped when he reached Ikuri. He swept up close, murmured "Is tonight okay?" and then quickly slipped away after seeing Ikuri nod. Afterwards the scent of machine oil lingered in the air. It was a nice smell.

She was happy that Akira had decided to come but she did not feel as excited as she thought she would. It was all the fault of that stupid leak. Her home was no longer the solid castle it used to be. It was fragile and insubstantial, not a place capable of safeguarding her secrets. How on earth could she embrace Akira without being conscious of what Takayama could hear in his apartment downstairs?

Ikuri returned home that evening at about six o'clock. A note had been stuffed in her doorjamb, but this time the same piece of paper was in everyone's door. It was a printed notice from the condominium corporation with the words Emergency Notification running across the top. It explained that specialists had been brought in to investigate the leak on the third floor but that the cause was still unclear. Other apartments also appeared to have leaks, so the crew urgently required access to all units not yet inspected. Residents were asked to remain at home tomorrow or to leave their key with the superintendent. If unable to comply, they were to indicate in writing a preferred date for the inspection and let the superintendent know. Inspection was scheduled for all day tomorrow and the day after, from 8:00 A.M. to 10:00 P.M.

It was terrible timing, but what could she do? At least they hadn't insisted on conducting the inspection tonight. She would ask them to come tomorrow evening. But nothing was going to change the hard truth that her building was falling apart.

She put her groceries in the fridge and took a quick shower. After that, there was nothing to do. She quietly got down on the carpet, stretched herself out and pressed her ear to the floor. For the past two nights this was where she had slept, not in her bed, which remained neat and undisturbed. Straight off she began straining intently for the faint sound of water dripping. When she was at last able to pick it out, the sense of relief she felt made her laugh. Yes, it had come to this. How could it be real? It had to be her imagination. And yet it sounded so real.

She strained to hear more. The dripping was heavier, no longer in just one spot but coming from all directions. Then there was a strange noise, the likes of which she had never heard before, a deep, low growl that rose in a sudden crescendo and ended in a deafening crash. Her immediate thought was that it must be an earthquake. She scrambled to her feet and looked around. The dull after-rumblings continued. How bizarre. Momentarily she entertained the notion that her entire building was collapsing.

At that moment the doorbell began ringing spasmodically, and thinking it must be Akira, she rushed to open the door. A frown crossed her face—it was Takayama. He forced his way in, squeezing his body forward. Ikuri unconsciously shrank back. A peculiar odor rose from his body.

"What's going on here? Let me see for myself!"

Ikuri made a futile attempt at blocking his way, but she didn't want to touch his body. Not only did he look extremely agitated, he was dripping wet. Drops of water fell from his clothes, staining Ikuri's entranceway.

"You're soaking wet," she said.

"Of course I am. Come down and you'll see. No, wait. What about here? Nothing's happening here?"

"No."

"How can that be!" Takayama's glazed eyes wandered unsteadily over the apartment until they came back to rest on Ikuri.

"What's the matter?" Ikuri could not retain her composure.

"Everything. Everything's a total mess." In an instant his arrogance dissolved without a trace. He puckered his face like he was ready to burst into tears.

"Please, I'm begging you. Come downstairs and take a look," he pleaded.

Water poured from the ceiling in a thin stream. This was no drip but a full-fledged shower, and puddles had formed throughout the room as if a storm had blown through. Part of the ceiling had split open about thirty centimeters, and strips of ripped wallpaper and chunks of plaster hung down from the hole.

"It was worse a minute ago. I thought the earth had ruptured. Who am I supposed to call for help? The Fire Department?"

Ikuri was so stunned by the incredible scene before her that she couldn't think straight. Takayama sounded exhausted. He snorted softly in derision at his own suggestion. "Ha, what a joke! A fire truck would only bring more water."

Where on earth was the water coming from? It had to be from somewhere above, but why wasn't there a single drop in her apartment? Ikuri stood transfixed. Merely gaping at the disaster was pointless, however, so she decided to pitch in and help. She ordered Takayama to gather as many towels and old sheets as he could spare and they spread them out on the floor to soak up the water. Then they hauled them into the bathroom to wring them out in the tub. They repeated this task over and over, going back and forth to the bathroom more times than they could count. In the end they mopped up enough water to fill a good third of the tub. As they worked, the stream of water from the ceiling began to subside until it was reduced to an occasional drip. During the whole time Takayama worked quietly without complaint.

When they were finished, they both collapsed wordlessly. As if poisonous water had been poured into the core of her body, Ikuri felt completely paralyzed.

Takayama ventured the first words. "It must be leaking like crazy below me. Good, let them have a taste of what it's like!" The units on the first and second floors were mainly used as offices.

Ikuri asked for the time, and Takayama motioned to the clock hanging on the wall. The hands pointed to 8:25.

"Nobody there now," he said. "They'll kick up a fuss in the morning."

She stood up and, rebuffing Takayama's entreaties to stay, rushed back to her own apartment.

Perhaps because her body was cold and wet, her apartment felt damp. To her bare feet, the carpet had an unpleasant chill and was buckled in a wavy pattern as if it had absorbed excess moisture. This was something new. Was it because of the flood downstairs? Ikuri was so tired she could only think of sleep. She took a long hot shower trying to warm her body, then collapsed on top of her bed.

Akira had probably come while she was downstairs. Come and gone. She had deliberately left her apartment door unlocked, but now she wondered whether he would have tried the doorknob. When she saw him at the plant tomorrow, she would apologize and explain. She even considered the possibility that he might be killing time somewhere, intending to come later tonight, but before she could finish the thought, she dropped off into a sound sleep.

She woke abruptly, startled that she'd fallen asleep without realizing it. How long had she been unconscious? Still only half awake, she wondered if continuing that descent into unconsciousness might not be what dying was like.

Something felt odd but she couldn't pinpoint quite what. Though she was exhausted, she was still wound up from the earlier events of the evening. She decided to wash up in the bathroom and force herself to go to sleep again. As she walked past the kitchen, she glanced up at the ceiling.

She stopped breathing. There was a pale, barely visible stain on the ceiling directly overhead, and in the middle of the stain a single transparent drop of water hung. It seemed to be getting bigger right before her eyes and looked like it might fall at any moment.

She started to scream and clapped a hand over her mouth. There was no one to hear her anyway. She was so tired she could barely focus, and everywhere she looked she saw double. She rubbed her eyes and looked again. Maybe the stain and the drop of water were an optical illusion. The longer she stared, the stiffer her neck became, the blurrier her vision.

She felt an overwhelming urge to run to Takayama for help. Her hand was on the doorknob, there was no time to think. Come what may, she knew she had to get out.

❧

Single Sickness

She dreamed you could see straight through her. One by one all the cells in her body were slowly floating to the surface of her skin where they burst into particles of light upon contact with the air. She was nothing more than an empty silhouette, barely recognizable as a human being. All that remained was a mesh of bright red blood vessels outlining the places where her organs and skin had once been.

Fukue protested vigorously against this sudden metamorphosis. How could she leave the house with her insides lit up and visible for all to see! She couldn't walk around like that. And despite all the holes in her body, there was no ventilation—it was still as stuffy as ever. Her body needed the cover of darkness again, that was all there was to it, or no one looking at her would know she was a person. Fine and dandy for her blood vessels to bask in the sun, but what about her, someone who used to have a full set of body organs. Now she was completely exposed, eviscerated. It was awful!

She woke herself up with her own angry ranting. It was after ten o'clock, and she hastened to get up from her futon, but the instant she did she felt something pulling her backwards. The next thing she knew her head was on the pillow again. Damn! Fukue suffered from chronic low blood pressure which meant she had frequent fainting spells, especially whenever she attempted to get up too quickly. For a few minutes she lay motionless with

51

her eyes closed to dispel the black clouds in her head, but by the time her dizziness had passed, so too had any desire to get out of bed. Just last night she'd composed her letter of resignation. What difference did it make if she was late for work? Sleeping in had probably been an unconscious act of protest.

The strong morning sun pouring through her green curtains had turned everything in her room, from her bedding to the walls, a dense opaque green. This same green light had passed through her eyelids, infiltrated her sleep, and made her see that pattern of red mesh. It was red because red was the complementary color of green. Fukue held her hand up towards the window. The light flickered like waves through her outspread fingers. Wasn't there a science fiction story about an invasion by space aliens who looked exactly like earthlings except their skin and blood were green?

The flickering motion of the light was beginning to make her feel seasick. The mere act of getting up from her futon had left her forehead damp with cold perspiration.

Fukue opened the curtains and a wave of bright sunlight crashed into the room. It was all she could do not to turn her head away. There it was, her letter of resignation, in the spot she had left it last night, neatly lined up next to her purse. She picked up her futon and sluggishly dragged it across the room and onto the balcony. As she hung it over the railing to air, she spotted an infant on the road directly below trying to walk by himself. He wobbled back and forth with each step, barely able to keep his balance, but he seemed singularly determined. There was no mother in sight anywhere. Fukue leaned over the balcony as far as she could to see if any cars were coming. The road had no sidewalk and depending on the time of day there could be quite a bit of traffic. Fortunately the infant managed to turn the corner before anything came along. At first Fukue waited for the child to start crying, but she didn't hear anything and she didn't feel like going down to see what had happened. It was the fault of the hot sun, she decided. It was baking every inch of her body, and now she realized that she honestly couldn't give a damn. She turned around and pressed her back against the futon, which hung over the railing. It had already started to fluff up in the heat of the sun. On a normal day, she wouldn't even be here, she reasoned, she'd have left for work long ago. That infant would have been walking on the road with the same determination.

Time itself seemed to drink in the hot sun, expanding and stretching before her very eyes. But the ribbon of time that stretched from infancy to her thirty-three years had at some point disintegrated into ragged flakes that now swirled in the sunlight. Even if she forced herself to be concerned about the fate of that child, it wouldn't last—there was nothing to support it. Even if she wanted to reach out, it was a waste of effort.

When she went back inside, the first thing that caught Fukue's eye was a black hair on her sheet. As soon as she picked it up, she noticed another and then another. She carefully combed the tatami mat until her fist was black with hair. The hairs—every strand had fallen from her own head—were covered with bits of white dust. In the strong sunlight, they looked filthy.

"Your resignation?" The Professor took the letter from Fukue without ceremony and smiled.

"That's right." Fukue smiled right back.

After a whole decade, it didn't seem real that she would soon be leaving for good. She boldly cast her eyes around her boss's office—she sure hadn't been invited in here in a long time. Without waiting to be asked, she sat down on the sofa and watched the Professor struggle to find his words.

"I suppose you have your reasons," he began tentatively. "I have no right to try to stop you."

"Correct."

It was hard to believe that this was her boss, this short pudgy man who picked his words so cautiously. He was clearly barely able to suppress a smirk. He was the only supervisor she'd had in her ten-year career at the Institute. If ever there was a relationship frozen in time, this was it.

"Is there anything you want to say to me before you leave?"

"Not a thing."

As long as he didn't ask her outright, there was no need for her to explain why she was quitting. No need to report that despite thinking about it long and hard last night, she didn't have a single concrete reason to offer. Once she was gone, Matsuki was certain to get her position as Senior Lecturer. At the time when he joined the Research Institute, there'd been no decent positions available and for the past three years, he'd been stuck as a lowly lab technician with a heavy workload. Apparently when he had come for his initial job interview, he'd been told something quite different. "The truth is I was promised your job. They were going to make you quit. But that was the last I heard of it." Matsuki had confided in Fukue once he realized that nothing was going to change.

"I wish I could say congratulations, but in your case ..." The Professor stood up, the signal that it was time for Fukue to leave.

She remained seated on the sofa. "Sorry, I don't understand."

"Well, it's clear you're not quitting to get married, are you. Look, if you haven't got anything else lined up, you can stay till you find another job."

Her resignation was such an unexpected windfall, the Professor could hardly contain his glee. Fukue had to hand it to him, there was something to envy about a man with such a childlike transparency. Somehow she felt like she was getting the short end of the stick.

"I had no idea marriage was cause for congratulations," she retorted, shooting him a look of withering contempt.

Instead of returning to her research lab, Fukue went up to the open concrete platform on the roof of the hospital. Nobody ever came here. It was extremely windy and smelled faintly of decaying organs and formaldehyde. The terrain in the area was very hilly and as a consequence anything up high was constantly windblown. There was so much wind that seen from above the cramped houses at the foot of the hospital always looked like they were shaking. The university and the affiliated teaching hospital where Fukue worked were built along the incline of a hill. In a way, everything was the fault of the hill because all floors could be entered directly from entrances along the slope. The first floor main entrance was at the base of the hill, the outpatients' reception was on the third floor level, and the university on the second. The research labs were in the basement. This was fine from the outside, but once inside it was all but impossible to find one's way around. Even a ten-year veteran like Fukue had never mastered the layout. To add to the confusion, additions built onto the hospital over the years were connected to the main structure by narrow high-walled passageways that ran underground. Most people, after going up and down a flight and making a few turns, got hopelessly lost. They didn't know which direction they faced or even what floor they were on. Although the research lab was nowhere near the clinical wing of the hospital, hardly a day went by that patients didn't get lost and stumble into the lab to ask for directions.

"You're killing mice!" they screamed when they found themselves face to face with staff in the midst of an experiment. It
had become Fukue's unofficial role to give these intruders a fierce
silent glare in return.

Looking down at the houses from her rooftop vantage point,
Fukue was prompted to think about all the people living inside or
scurrying back and forth along the street. One part of her wondered why she hadn't left her job a decade ago, why she'd held on
all these years, but if so, then another part wondered why she had
given in to sudden impulse last night. After all, she had no idea
what she was going to do next. Gusts of wind tugged on her white
lab coat and mussed her hair. It felt good but it also felt as if every
thought in her head was being blown away. This wind could sweep
her high in the air, then drop her somewhere far away. Drop her
down so hard she would smash into granules of powder.

All of the mice under Fukue's care were doing extremely well.
She poked their bellies with her finger to monitor the progress of
the distinct hard lumps that were now large enough to protrude
through the abdominal wall. Their fur was falling out in patches
and the downy hair that coated their undersides had turned yellow. The lumps—she knew they were bona fide cancer tumors—
were developing nicely with each passing day. After confirming the
presence of cancer through biopsies, Fukue then injected extracts
of the diseased tissue into a different set of healthy mice. This
second generation of mice now crouched listlessly at the back of
their cages. They too had cancer.

Fukue had succeeded in triggering the growth of cancerous
cells using a radical new method of her own devising. In contrast
to the standard methods used to stimulate cancer in animals—
brushing nicotine tar on their fur or pumping their lungs full of

cigarette smoke—Fukue's technique was very primitive. Everyday for two hours she took the sharp tip of her ballpoint pen and jabbed her mice in every conceivable spot all over their bodies. What she wanted to know was if tumors would develop in tissue subjected to the stress of continual harassment. Sure enough, after six months, half of her original ten mice displayed signs of abnormality: lethargy, violence, cannibalism, hair loss, color change. Finally, two developed cancer. She'd done it!—harassment as a new kind of carcinogen. In a decade of working at the Institute, it was her first and only success.

"You've proven your cancer, you don't need the mice anymore. Why not put them down?" said the handler whose job it was to breed and care for the experimental mice. "Put yourself in my shoes. Even if it's for the sake of science, who can bear to watch them suffer day and night." He smiled and pressed his hands against his chest. Rumor had it that any scientist who didn't come to the lab regularly to check the mice in his experiments might find a sudden and inexplicable jump in deaths from "natural causes." Because Fukue had to visit the lab daily to personally administer her "treatments," she hadn't lost a single mouse so far. Not even among those with cancer.

"Aren't you interested in knowing how long they can survive?" she said. "Even after they die, we can extract live cancer cells from them. Anyway, they're already goners. Why should I go to the trouble of killing them?"

"Killing, killing—stop it! You scientists get a kick out of giving them incurable diseases. It's different for me. I raised them with my own hands."

Of course Fukue had never set out to cure anything. Medicine was strange that way. The goal was to take an incurable disease and turn it into a minor ailment. At least among Fukue's colleagues at the lab, not a single one of them understood the concept of "cure." And she was no better, devising new and different ways to make perfectly healthy, active mice sick. The optimistic premise upon which everything rested was that understanding how to cause disease was the key to finding the cure, and that became her defense. But Fukue suspected that psychological testing would confirm there were proportionally more sadists among medical researchers than in the general population. She herself had no intention of reporting the results of her experiment to her boss. Instead she planned to publish an article in one of his favorite medical journals.

People and animals shared the same natural instinct for aggression and bullying. If caged together too long, lab mice did not develop closer bonds. Quite the contrary, they ate each other up.

"Listen, I'll be quitting soon. I'll take care of them before I leave." Saying this out loud made her resignation seem just a little more concrete. But the breeder was indifferent. "Either way," he muttered, shaking his head as he walked away. "They won't live much longer." Psychological testing of his profession would surely confirm a strong masochistic streak.

One of Fukue's cancer-riddled mice stood up on its hind legs in the corner of the cage, its long white claws clinging fiercely to the fine wire mesh at the bottom. Either way. If the mouse could talk, it would surely second that sentiment. For a brief moment Fukue and the mouse stared straight into each other's eyes. She smiled uneasily.

"Either way, you're gonna die, so you might as well have cancer," she said. "At least you're doing something. Listen, I'm just one of billions of human beings born without purpose, but you're special. We made you and gave you a specific purpose. So don't dwell on why you have to suffer like this. It's all because of me. I decided to put cancer in your body, just on a whim. We human beings live well over seventy years, and it's all we can do to keep thinking up new projects so we won't go crazy with boredom."

As if the words were covered with rust, they snagged in her throat and tumbled out in spurts. The words rained down on the mouse, who continued to stare intently up at her.

Fukue had started at the Pathology Research Institute ten years ago as an entry-level lab technician. The job was to help with the experiments, and she got the position through her old college professor's connections. That meant the job interview had been a mere formality.

At the time of the interview, the man who had hired her, the Assistant Professor, gave her a warning. "If anyone tries to bully you, don't put up with it. Come straight to me."

What a strange place to work, she thought, but at the time she couldn't afford to be choosy. The economy was in a slump and she had no other prospects. Once she started, she discovered that her real job was to sit in her boss's office and listen to his complaints all day long. Whenever she emerged from his office, the other researchers would pounce. "You poor thing, locked up like a prisoner in there," they said. "What kind of nasty things has he been telling you about us?"

It didn't take long for Fukue to figure out that she'd landed smack in the middle of a political storm involving promotion. At the center of the maelstrom was her boss who, she learned, was considered totally incompetent. Apparently no one thought he stood any chance of garnering enough votes in the academic election to be promoted to full Professor. Work in the lab had ground to a standstill as speculation rose about who might be brought in from the outside as the new Director.

"We don't care if you're a stoolie," her co-workers taunted. "Go ahead and tell him everything we say. Don't leave out a word."

While the Assistant Professor hid in his office, refusing to set foot in the laboratory, his superior, the most senior Professor at the Institute, had stopped coming in entirely. He cited health reasons but rumor had it that the old professor couldn't stand his underling's tears and hysterics. Meanwhile, no one would explain to Fukue what she was supposed to do in the lab. In her boss's office, she had to listen to him brag about his studies in America or complain about the other researchers. He told her what a big role she was going to play under him in the new organization. The elections were fast approaching.

"Damn them all! Why did they pick this year to change the system? I never heard of anything so stupid. All my predecessors were promoted on the basis of recommendations from their supervisors, but mine is too 'noble' for that. He's supposed to recommend me but he's too busy at home calculating his pension earnings. What the hell is going to happen to me!"

To Fukue's horror, her balding middle-aged boss—he was well over fifty—suddenly began blubbering.

"If I'm forced out, you'll come with me, won't you?" Tears rolled down the cheeks of his plump white face as he reached forward to grab Fukue's hands.

"Where would you go?" she asked, quickly thrusting her hands behind her back.

"How should I know? I can't stay here!" His outstretched hands dangled awkwardly in mid-air. At a loss for what to do, he began clasping and unclasping them between his knees.

"Come on, let's get out of here together," he urged.

"Not me!" Fukue was shocked by the coldness in her voice.

That put an abrupt end to her visits. Her colleagues in the lab mistakenly assumed she had chosen to side with them. They attempted to engage her in their gossip.

"Would someone mind explaining what my job is supposed to be?" she asked.

"Forget about work, there's no point until after this storm passes. You really had a lot of patience putting up with him this long."

"But I really want to work."

"Well, no one's stopping you. Surely you must have learned everything there is to know in your private sessions with you-know-who. Anyway, we're under strict orders and can't ask you to do anything without permission."

Fukue devised her own daily routine of study in the library. Although she didn't even know the main research themes of the lab, she conducted document searches and translated foreign language articles into Japanese. Sitting in the empty library, she sometimes felt like she was being held hostage by madmen. She wanted to scream out loud. Who gives a damn about who becomes Professor!

Fukue's appointment to such a prestigious academic research institute had made her the envy of her friends and classmates. How ironic it would be if, after the voting was over, she turned out to be the first to lose her job.

But the tempest came and went, and in the end Fukue's boss received his promotion, squeaking through by one vote.

"It's all politics."

"They were afraid of an outsider. The insider was a safer bet."

"I thought things would turn out like this."

All the senior researchers had clearly made contingency plans and one by one they left for other positions. Before she knew it,

Fukue was the only "survivor" left behind. In no time she became the most senior researcher and her status rose accordingly with an automatic promotion first to Research Associate and then to Senior Lecturer. With the employment market so tight, she was well aware that as a recent graduate without special connections she couldn't afford to sneer at a job in hand.

New researchers were hired, and they treated Fukue with the same deference as they did the Professor. How could they possibly know that the sum total of her knowledge consisted of what she'd been able to pick up from her days spent in the library or from snooping around the desktops of her former colleagues? To assert her authority, she hid the chemical reagents needed for the experiments so she would be the only one who could find them quickly. This was her way of standing up not only to the newcomers but also their boss. He'd been away from the lab for so long he didn't know where anything was. The fact that the Professor ignored Fukue's research and never included her in any committees must have puzzled the new staff, but they seemed to assume it was the prerogative of her senior status and they were more careful than ever to treat her politely. Fukue resolved that if the Professor let his dislike of her get out of hand, she was prepared to remind him of the nostalgic "good old days" when she first came here.

Two important teaching positions remained unfilled, and the new staff were left to muddle along on their own individual projects without proper guidance. Although this situation continued for several years, not a single person quit.

Normally Fukue went home before Matsuki, but the following evening he hung up his lab coat as soon as he saw her preparing to leave. Together they walked to the train station. The sound of Matsuki's footsteps beside her made Fukue feel like she was saddled with a heavy weight that slowed her down.

The surplus weight beside her spoke. "What are you going to do now? Personally I think he's the one who should leave, not you. He's thirty years older, he's ready to retire. Anyway, it's the university we work for, not him. There's a tendency to forget that."

Matsuki had been hired four years ago while he was still working on his Master's degree. Only twenty-seven years old, he was still a good forty years from retirement. Fukue couldn't help laughing.

"Hey, I'm not joking!" Matsuki put out his fist to cover her mouth. At the station people were crowded around the ticket gates. "I didn't come here to be his servant," he continued. "I came here to conduct research. To me the place is more important than the people, although of course I can't help thinking about when he'll retire."

Matsuki pushed into the crowd, holding his arms out to break the way for Fukue.

What kind of future would Matsuki have? It didn't matter that he had determination. As far as Fukue could tell, unless you had the proper degree—a medical degree—researchers didn't last here past the age of thirty-five. They were usually forced to find jobs elsewhere, and once they were gone, nobody seemed to care what had become of them.

"I'm worried about you," Matsuki said. "You're not suited to do anything else except work in a research lab. I hate to see you run away just because you don't get along with the boss. I'm against women throwing away their scientific education for such a stupid reason. What kind of message is that for the next generation of women."

Fukue smiled at Matsuki. She had a momentary hallucination of herself as the illustrious woman of science stepping down after her ten-year career to make way for the younger generation. Looking into his eyes, she saw the reflection of a confident woman who had carefully considered all these matters before writing her letter of resignation.

"Don't you think it's interesting that for all our scientific knowledge people are still dying of starvation? What does that say about the fate of mankind? Maybe we spend too much time in our ivory tower, maybe we're too spoiled by freedom. Oh, by the way, once you've been a Senior Lecturer for three years, you've earned the qualifications to write your thesis. Usually that's about seven years. Anyway, the rules are the rules."

"Three years ... Really?"

"That's right. Hey, only three years."

Matsuki's eyes fluttered upwards.

They began moving again, shoved forward by the people behind them. Adept at picking her way through the crowds, Fukue charged ahead at full speed. If Matsuki couldn't keep up with her, well, that was too bad. The train car was jam-packed.

It was the first time Matsuki had spoken so frankly, and Fukue wondered if by voicing his convictions aloud, he thought the sheer force of his words could propel him through the next forty years until retirement. Fukue had chosen silence, but it had only served her for ten years.

On her way home Fukue stopped at her local vegetable store where cardboard boxes were always piled in front of the shop at the end of the day. She pointed her finger at them.

"Do you need some boxes?" The owner's wife selected four boxes, flattened them and tied up with string.

"Are you moving?"

Fukue shook her head ambiguously and smiled. She began counting out some change.

"Oh, that's not necessary. We throw them out. The only time we charge for boxes is when people are moving because we're losing a customer. Can you manage all of them?"

The woman seemed to be under the impression that Fukue was mute because she never spoke. Instead of asking for things, Fukue simply pointed at whenever she wanted, exaggerating her facial expressions and gestures to compensate for her silence. People always thought the best of you if you didn't talk, and she hadn't had a single bad experience at any of her neighborhood shops. The indefinable sense of anxiety that swilled around inside her had a tendency to spill out if she had to make conversation. So at some point she'd hit upon the audacious strategy of making the other person do all the talking. Nod. Shake your head. Tilt it to the side. As long as there was a smiling face on top of your neck, no one ever forced you to speak. There was no shortage of talkative people who wanted an audience for their endless complaints.

The boxes were heavier than Fukue thought and by the time she'd dragged them up the narrow staircase to her apartment, she was drenched in sweat. While she waited for the water to heat so she could take a sponge bath, she did a quick mental calculation of the books that lined three walls of her apartment. No, four cardboard boxes were definitely not enough. She decided to call a used book dealer this Sunday and sell her books, most of which were specialized academic texts. Contemplating her next step would be easier once the books were out of the way. For the past ten years, the apartment had been little more than a study carrel, a place for her desk and her books.

Thanks to all the time she had spent with her nose in her books, when Fukue heard the word "human being," she automatically visualized cross-sections of the brain or full-body anatomy charts. "Life" was the biological process initiated by the union of sperm and egg, and "death" the ultimate aging of cells and disintegration of body organs. Human beings were nothing more than a bunch of molecules and enzymes moving systematically along the conveyor belts of the body's factory. Raw materials were burned, energy was produced. The Professor, Matsuki, and Fukue herself were biochemical compounds made from exactly the same "raw materials" using exactly the same "manufacturing process-es." But there was something about summing up a human being this way that sometimes made her brain lock down. Her books might contain the crystallization of intellectual achievement, but perhaps they were also to blame for repressing the wild, unpredict-able urges in her heart.

If she allowed herself to be convinced that human existence was absurd and unknowable, then what did that say about her own existence. The textbooks never talked about things like why you feel bad when you're covered in sweat or when you might be struck with the impulse to resign your job. Fukue poured boiling water into a washbasin and took off her top. Before adding cold water to cool it off, she dipped her fingers in the hot water and touched her breasts. Enough of being so boring! She'd do whatever she wanted.

Matsuki would never rise to the level of full Professor, no matter how long he worked. The best he could hope for might be an academic appointment at a junior college or women's univer-sity, and even that would require a lot of kowtowing to his supe-rior and producing a pile of research. Maybe he could manage it in ten years. Of course, if he stayed at the Institute, as he insisted he wanted to, he would become just another one of the obsequi-ous instructors there. Matsuki wasn't genius material or even a particularly sharp thinker, and while it wasn't possible to expect a future beyond the talents bestowed on you by nature, Matsuki was afraid to dream of anything slightly out of reach. His type couldn't start even the smallest of revolutions. In fact, it didn't matter if he existed or not.

Fukue wiped her chest with a damp towel. She still couldn't get over how she'd given in to impulse and handed in her resignation. That was quite a feat for her. She liked this new self—this unpredictable self—and she looked forward to developing it. It was bound to be more fun than the old self.

Suddenly she groaned. She lifted the now cold towel from her left breast—her flesh was covered with goose bumps—and pressed again in the same spot. She felt a sharp, shooting pain. She let go of the towel and began palpating her entire breast with her fingers. A faint blue vein ran through the white skin of her breast directly over the spot where it hurt.

The pages of her medical textbook with its colored cross-sectional diagrams came into her head, especially the pictures of the breast divided into quadrants. Her mind froze. Fukue's pain was located in the outer-lower quadrant near the armpit, the quadrant where cancer most often developed.

"It's small, about the size of an azuki bean. I'm surprised you could feel anything." Dr. Niki, the doctor on duty in the outpatient clinic, smiled as he pressed gently on Fukue's breast with his index and middle fingers. Fukue had tried doing her own self-examination but she hadn't been able to locate the lump.

"Possibly nothing will show, but let's have a mammogram taken," he said.

Fukue made her way down the narrow, dimly lit underground passage and followed the green line on the floor to the Medical Imaging Department. She felt acutely self-conscious in her white lab coat. Hospital staff received preferential treatment for medical tests taken during working hours and were immediately pushed ahead of everyone else to the head of the line. It was the hospital's way of ensuring that its staff got back to their jobs as quickly as possible.

The radiologist was a young woman. "What a surprise to see my old teacher!" she exclaimed. "What are you here for?"

Two or three years ago the woman had taken a practicum in pathology with Fukue who recalled having to reprimand her for trying to make the male students do all the work.

"I think this is it." The radiologist squeezed Fukue's breast hard and squashed it into position.

"Please get it over with," Fukue snapped. "I haven't got all day."

"Almost done. By the way, are you married?"

"No."

"I didn't mean in the literal sense. I meant are you ... well, you know ... "

"Look, Dr. Niki is handling my case."

The female flesh under her hospital gown suddenly struck Fukue as very depressing. She'd already been through all these questions in the clinic. Is your period regular? Are you single? Are you married?

The radiologist gave Fukue a copy of the mammogram to carry back to Dr. Niki. "Remember, there's no point in worrying until you get the final results."

There wasn't much to the mammogram, just the faint semi-circle outline of a breast. For this she'd had to take off her clothes in front of a former student. Dr. Niki booked her for an ultrasound test in two days.

Close to a hundred people were sitting in the outpatient lobby waiting for their names to be called. They'd been there for hours.

When Fukue emerged from the clinic wearing her lab coat, everyone turned to look at her, their eyes filled with frustration. Fukue walked through the crowd briskly, unconsciously sticking out her chest. Fine, she thought, let them think she was a doctor if they wanted.

Fukue found herself straining to recall exactly what the metabolism map of the breast had looked like in her textbooks. But she couldn't bring herself to open any of those books, just as she couldn't bear to ask Dr. Niki outright if she had cancer. Dr. Niki was the breast cancer specialist at the hospital, so he'd seen more than enough. How could she ask someone like that: "Doctor, is it cancer? Tell me, is it cancer?" It was too embarrassing. Not only that, Dr. Niki had just returned from a Cambodian refugee camp where he had led the government-sponsored medical mission from their hospital. For the three months he was there, he'd treated hundreds of patients on the verge of death.

All she had was a little "azuki bean." If it turned out to be cancerous, then the solution was simple—cut off her breast. It wasn't life threatening. After all, Dr. Niki had been smiling when he examined her.

Her breasts—they hadn't been much use to her so far. For that matter, maybe she should have both of them taken care of at the same time.

Back at her desk, Fukue began sorting through her papers and making a pile of important documents. In the late afternoon Matsuki came by and invited her up to the rooftop.

"I was told to be patient and wait a bit longer," he said bitterly.

A thought came to Fukue out of the blue. A woman didn't need breasts for herself. She needed them for men! Fukue wondered if Matsuki had ever fondled a woman's breasts.

"When I tell you his excuse, you'll laugh." Matsuki tried laughing himself but his strained expression looked like it might collapse into tears at any moment.

All Matsuki wanted to talk about was the position of Senior Lecturer, her position. It made Fukue suddenly think about medical expenses. What if she needed surgery? As an employee, medical treatment was either free or less than half the normal fee. But in a month's time she would no longer be on staff. No benefits, no supplementary insurance coverage. Until now she hadn't even needed cold medication. She looked at Matsuki's strapping physique. He was the picture of health.

"Oh, don't worry, he said," Matsuki continued. "It's so ridiculous I didn't even feel like putting up an argument."

The cold wind bit straight through Fukue's lab coat to her breast.

"Can't mention any names," Matsuki mimicked the Professor's voice, "but in the past there was someone who stopped producing work after getting promoted. We can't be too careful."

Matsuki went over to the iron railing. "He must hate me, plain and simple. How else to explain the way I've been treated. I've been here four years."

"Why don't you say you'll do whatever he wants to make him like you," Fukue said.

Matsuki glared at her, but he didn't say he'd rather quit. He said, "I'm worried about my future."

He didn't seem to understand that there'd be no more promotions after he became Senior Lecturer. He was better off stretching out the pleasure of anticipation.

"Didn't you say your loyalty was to the place, not the people."

"I did. But it's people who make the place. I guess I'm capricious."

"Now you're talking." Fukue laughed and looked down over the railing. "Stick it out as long as you can and when you can't stand it anymore, don't. Seeing someone who tries too hard would make anyone feel like making fun."

"I'm not a child."

"What would you do if I said I'm taking back my resignation?"

Even if Matsuki was groveling, she shouldn't be so mean. But everything about him smacked of such moral rectitude, it brought out the worst in her.

"It's up to you," he said, but Fukue could see his shoulders droop visibly. "I didn't ask to be made Senior Lecturer. It's the principle. I don't like the way things are done around here. And to set the record straight, I'm not trying to make you like me either."

"Well, it's not easy to make him like you. The Boss once told me there are two things you have to put up with—the work and the workers. When both of them start to get to you, it's time to go."

"What you had to 'put up' with was another worker, right?

"That's right, you."

They both fell silent. For Fukue it was easy being with someone who was so narcissistic, she could relax and forget about him.

What good was having a brain if it didn't know what was going on in the rest of the body. All this time Fukue's cerebral cortex had been blithely unaware of the abnormal activity bubbling up in her breast. How stupid and useless the whole central nervous system was. Fukue squashed her breast hard against the iron railing, but the pain had mysteriously vanished. She groped her body in a kind of panic.

She was not afraid of dying, even if her courage came from knowing that she probably wasn't in any real danger. The worst part was not being able to see with her own eyes the deadly cells growing deep inside her. Like Matsuki, the source of her anxiety was the formless, intangible "unknown."

As far as Fukue was concerned, it was a foregone conclusion that Matsuki would be promoted to Senior Lecturer after she left, even if the matter seemed far from resolved to either Matsuki or the Professor. There was one other absolute certainty in her mind: the tumor lurking in her breast. Let them probe and examine it any way they liked, its essential immutable nature was already fixed. It was just waiting to be discovered. Maybe Dr. Niki already had.

Dr. Niki was waiting in the examination room when Fukue arrived for her ultrasound. She lay back on the examination table, and he put some transparent jelly on her left breast. With the palm of his hand he rubbed her breast in a rotating motion like a massage until he had spread the jelly evenly. Fukue felt a cold heaviness, like an icepack, on her breast, followed immediately by the sudden return of a fiery pain.

Dr. Niki's bare hand on her breast had felt nice. It was the healing hand of a middle-aged surgeon who had touched hundreds of burnt, torn, disfigured breasts in the Cambodian refugee camp. Letting a man touch her breast hadn't been as bad as she'd imagined.

"I once had a young female patient."

Unexpectedly Dr. Niki's soothing voice rose over the low hum of the ultrasound machine. Fukue opened her eyes to see Dr. Niki crouched in an awkward pose, half-sitting and half-standing, with his arms stretched out. One hand was on the machine dials and the other was on the "icepack." His eyes were fixed intently on the screen.

"She had gotten it into her head that she had cancer of the uterus. No matter how many times I told her she didn't, she wouldn't believe me. She kept saying, 'I beg you to tell me the truth. If it's cancer I'm going to jump out the window.' I repeated that what she had was inflammation of the uterine muscle tissue, not cancer, but to no avail. She called me a liar. She was bent on being told she had cancer and throwing herself from the eighth floor of the hospital."

Fukue observed the doctor's profile. His lips were pursed tightly shut and he gave no sign of talking more. She forced a light laugh to encourage him to continue. "And then?"

"The previous year the woman had lost first her father and then her younger brother," Dr. Niki resumed. "Her father died of stomach cancer, the brother of acute intestinal obstruction, as I recall. They were the only family she had. How about you? Do you have family?"

"No—"

"I see." Without asking for clarification, Dr. Niki continued. "I told her to come back after she'd been seen by a psychiatrist, and she accused me of wanting her to die. By then it would be too late to treat her cancer. In the end, I lost my temper. 'If you prefer your own diagnosis, believe whatever you want. Go ahead and jump.' I thought she would try to leap out the window right then and there in front of me. Instead she burst into tears and suddenly became extremely docile. We were tremendously relieved, so what happened was all the more a shame ..."

"She jumped after all?"

"No, someone else did. Another woman in the same ward. Right after it happened, my patient went back to normal."

"A different woman!"

"Yes. That patient really did have uterine cancer although we hadn't told her yet. It was a tragedy because her cancer was definitely treatable. I guess hysteria is contagious."

Dr. Niki switched off the ultrasound machine and carefully wiped the jelly from Fukue's breast.

"You can get dressed now."

Fukue got up as instructed. After the story he'd just told her, she thought she should make a joke. Something like, hey Doc, what about me?

Dr. Niki rolled up the data printout and stuffed it into the pocket of his lab coat.

"It will be a small excision, but we need to perform a biopsy," he said. "We won't know anything until we've analyzed a tissue sample."

He didn't use the word cancer, he didn't say anything about what he'd seen on her mammogram or ultrasound. But Fukue knew that biopsies were conducted when the suspicion of malignancy was strong.

"I understand you're a pathology specialist. Do you want to examine the tissue yourself?"

So he knew who she was.

"No, thanks. I'd better pass. I couldn't trust myself."

"How about early next week?"

Smiling—what else could she do—Fukue nodded in assent.

A rumor started circulating in the Lab that Matsuki was about to quit. As yet though, no one except Matsuki and the Professor seemed to know anything about Fukue's resignation.

"Matsuki's going around saying that he'll quit if I don't promote him. Just as I've always thought, he's a real disappointment." The Professor had abruptly summoned Fukue to his office.

For a moment Fukue thought he was about to say, "I'm firing Matsuki. You've got to stay on!"

Instead he continued, "Tell Matsuki if he feels like quitting, he should quit, but if he has a grievance, he should see me directly. I don't recall ever saying I wouldn't appoint him as a lecturer."

"Perhaps you should tell him yourself," she said. "I don't know anything about it."

As in the past, as soon as she was in the Professor's office, Fukue felt desperate to escape. The man was so insecure he always needed at least one enemy—real or imagined—to fight.

"Excuse me, I thought there might be a connection to your resignation. I can't make personal deals, you see. We should employ proper methods, it's in everyone's best interests. I don't mind having an eccentric around, but that Matsuki, he's becoming a troublemaker."

Fukue smiled wickedly as she recalled the Professor's tear-streaked face when he was so frantic about his own promotion. Could he read her thoughts? He stared up at the ceiling intently.

"Matsuki's a good person, of course," he said with a tight smile. Abruptly, he changed the topic. "I hear you're being seen at the hospital."

How on earth did he know? Although he rarely left his office, he seemed to have eyes and ears were everywhere, skillfully extracting information from the people who worked for him. Fukue had the uneasy feeling that at any moment he might lean forward and slap his pudgy hand on her breast. Her whole body stiffened.

"No," she replied. The word stuck on the roof of her mouth like a ball of thick mucous.

"I'm relieved to hear that. But I'd advise getting a full medical before you leave. It will be your last chance to take advantage of employee benefits. Otherwise you'll find it's very expensive."

Matsuki was waiting for Fukue in the researchers' office.

"You got a call saying one of your mice died," he said. "It's in the freezer waiting for you to dissect later. The breeder sounded especially menacing. 'One's dead, the others aren't far behind.' I'd say the sooner you see him the better. He might just do it, you know."

Everyday the breeder kept an anxious watch over dying animals, so small wonder he had developed an abiding hatred of the scientists. His retaliation was to put the mice out of their misery himself. Fukue couldn't help wondering what he thought about the terminally ill patients moaning in pain at the other end of the building.

"I'll look after it," she said. "By the way, I heard you'll be getting your promotion. I'm not sure why he told me."

"The boss?"

"Uh huh."

Watching Matsuki's face slowly brighten, Fukue couldn't help thinking how this Lab operated in perfect running order.

"But why all of a sudden ...?" Matsuki muttered to himself. His voice had a pleased, coquettish tone.

She merely shrugged her shoulders.

Fukue was not the squeamish type, and it didn't bother her in the least to slice open the diseased body of a dead mouse. The mice were supposed to die—it was as natural as natural could be. But even she nearly lost her grip on her surgical shears when she encountered a belly full of little babies. The fetuses were tiny, measuring only a centimeter in length. In the animal world, the female always became a mother. If Fukue's breasts were cut off, would it mean never knowing life "as a woman"? Why was it that she had never known love, not even once? That the only man to touch her breast was a doctor performing a medical procedure. How could anyone have been too busy to experience love?

One by one she methodically removed each of the mouse's internal organs and the fingertip-size fetuses. Each organ, she knew, served its own unique function in the body. Glistening wet and pink, the now empty abdominal cavity struck her as extremely erotic.

Once Fukue had sold her books, the stains on her apartment walls were exposed, and a dark wide shadow circled the room in the places where her books had stood. This dismal cave was where she had lived, counting off the days one after the other. She didn't know any of her neighbors and might as well have been living in a ghost town for all the human contact she had.

She thought of a river running through the middle of a vast parched field, a river moving steadily without pause but so slowly it made no sound. As it flowed, it carried silt from the bottom of the river and deposited it at the river's mouth until a huge mountain of mud eventually blocked the flow. For the river to move again, for the mountain of mud to be blasted aside, it required nothing less than a gigantic flood. Who knew where those rushing torrents of water might go.

Fukue recalled Dr. Niki's story about the patient who was convinced she had uterine cancer. What would she do if her cancer was terminal? What kind of a torrent would she create? Would she wail hysterically? Nod calmly in quiet resignation? Would she want to kill her doctor? Would she scream, "No, no! I want to live longer!" To Fukue her breasts were useless, alien things whose original purpose was to feed a stranger, a hypothetical baby. Why should her life be threatened by something so irrelevant to her existence? Or was it really her life itself that was irrelevant?

At her next appointment, Fukue was greeted not by Dr. Niki but by another doctor, an arrogant man who also lectured in the medical school.

"Isn't Dr. Niki here today?" she inquired politely.

"It doesn't look like it, does it," the doctor replied aggressively. Reassuring herself that it didn't matter—she was here to set a date for her upcoming biopsy—Fukue went behind the curtain, took off her top, and lay down on the examination table. Just as Dr. Niki had instructed her the previous time, she turned her body at a slight angle to raise her left side and lifted her arm over her head. But the new doctor shoved her flat. He pinched her breast hard handling it in the same rough way as the former student who had taken her mammogram. Fukue scrunched up her face in an effort not to yelp out loud with pain.

"There's no point in doing a biopsy," the doctor curtly announced at the end of the examination. "There's nothing in your breast."

"But Dr. Niki said he felt something the size of an azuki bean."

"Well, there's nothing there, believe me. If there were, I'd be more than happy to cut it out for you." With that the doctor again pressed his fingers even deeper into her breast. Fukue felt certain he had squished her tumor so hard it had burst open and sent bits of cancerous debris flying throughout her body.

"Could it disappear just like that?" she asked.

"Come on. Forget about it."

The doctor briskly stepped outside the curtain. Where he'd examined Fukue's breast there was now a reddish bruise. She thought about coming back again on a day when Dr. Niki would be on duty, but she didn't have much time left. Hurriedly buttoning up her lab coat, Fukue hastened after the doctor.

"I really do feel pain, you know, and the left breast is definitely more swollen than the other. It feels heavier. I insist that you tell me what condition I've got."

Without even bothering to look up from the chart in which he was writing, the doctor replied. "Mastitis. A breast abscess."

"Will it get better on its own?"

"If it's unbearable I can give you a needle. If you're worried about it, come back in one or two months."

"I can't afford to have it get worse."

Dr. Niki had been so thorough, Fukue couldn't imagine him dismissing the possibility of cancer just like that. He was still her attending physician, wasn't he? He had yet to give her his final diagnosis. Besides, what was mastitis? She'd never heard of it before.

The doctor looked extremely irritated when Fukue made no move to leave the examination room.

"Want to know the best cure," he said. "Get married and have a baby."

"What!"

"You're keeping your breasts to yourself, that's the problem. The mammary glands need exercise, so have a baby. Producing milk is one of the best ways to soften and heal the tissue. When women don't perform the duties nature assigned them, this is what happens—they get punished with things like mastitis or uterine inflammation. Face it, Dr. Niki was just being excessively cautious with you because he knew you're a pathology specialist."

As soon as she left the doctor's office, Fukue headed straight for the library and looked up mastitis. Treatment included injections of male hormones. But the entry also said that the only definitive way to rule out cancer was to take a tissue biopsy.

It wasn't until several days later that Fukue learned Dr. Niki had been admitted to hospital. She came upon Matsuki and the

Professor having tea in one of the staff rooms. As she stood at the doorway and stared in astonishment, Matsuki looked away and continued talking.

"I heard those refugee camps are filthy. Some of the nurses on the mission got infected, too. That's a fine 'thank you' for all the help they gave. I'm sure others will stop and think twice before signing up for a relief mission."

The Professor spoke. "Just the other day, a neurotic seventy-eight year old woman decided to do away with herself by jumping into the river. A nineteen year old boy plunged in to save her and ended up drowning. The old lady survived. Doesn't that remind you of Niki? He's just like that boy, full of heroics and compassion. But make no mistake, he's got his eye on his own research, too. Going over there was a good chance to see diseases that don't exist in Japan anymore. Don't tell me that wasn't his real motive."

With both the Professor and Fukue watching him, Matsuki didn't know how to respond. He gave a noncommittal "aaah."

"They complain that Japan isn't doing enough, so we immediately jump up and join the relief efforts. It's a knee-jerk reaction. They won't let us get out of war. No, we have to sweat it out in relief missions. Well, you won't find me going on any of those missions. That's putting the cart before the horse. When you bring back something as infectious as hepatitis B, you cause everyone nothing but trouble."

"Dr. Niki is pretty ill, isn't he," Matsuki said. Only a few months earlier, he had gushed with envy when he read an article about Dr. Niki's relief mission in the university bulletin.

Fukue managed to catch up with Matsuki later. "When did Dr. Niki go into hospital?" It turned out it was one or two days after her ultrasound.

"Do you know him?" Matsuki asked, again trying to curry favor.

"I do indeed," she replied smugly. "I'd better pay him a visit right away."

All her mice were dead. The cause, she was told, was an outbreak of pneumonia, and she didn't bother doing any autopsies. With only two weeks left, Fukue decided to use up her remaining vacation time to clean her apartment. Then one day she suddenly realized that her last official day on the job had come and gone. As if seized with a fit, she grabbed her suitcase and dashed out the door, making a beeline for the train station. The sun was so strong it burnt deep into her back and penetrated her whole body. It felt as if the sun were loosening the cells—all her cells—the good, healthy cells and the other cells filled with garbage, setting them free to swirl upwards on their own towards the source of light and heat. Wasn't "living" simply the daily accumulation of more and more garbage in the body? Every single day in the human and animal world, creatures were born and passed away, one number canceling out the other in a perfect balance of infinity. Fukue was just one of that infinite number, and eventually she, too, would dissolve into garbage. At the present moment, though, she didn't know where she was headed and it made her feel strangely buoyant and giddy. She jumped on the first train that came into the station and looking out the window, she was blinded by the dazzling sunlight. The people and streets were all shadowy silhouettes.

∾

Horn

Horn: term used for hard, pointed projections growing from the heads of mammals. Also used in reference to similar growths on nonmammals. Considerable variety in structure and composition, ranging from solid to hollow to complex branched structures. Composed primarily of one of two main substances—keratin (protein found in hair, nails, beaks) or calcium (essential component of bones). Function chiefly as weapons, but in some cases develop as secondary sexual characteristics.

People are mammals, I reasoned, so why shouldn't a person have horns? Why should it only be demons? Of course, we have the "horn-hiding" hood, the *tsunokakushi* headpiece used in traditional wedding ceremonies, but apparently it had nothing to do with horns originally. It's just a carryover from ancient times when women were supposed to keep everything—their faces, names, and personalities—hidden from sight. Two of my girlfriends were married wearing the *tsunokakushi,* and while they don't have sharp horns to hide, I'll admit they both have sharp tongues. They told me it took them twenty years to finally be able to stand up to their mothers-in-law. But compare that to our other friends who got married in Western wedding gowns—so far not one of them dares talk back.

I wanted to know under what circumstances a person might sprout a horn, but no matter how many books I've consulted, I can't find a single word on the topic. I should explain that my own horn is not the sort of grand affair that would require an elaborate horn-hiding hood for concealment. It's a pretty puny specimen, easily covered with a single adhesive bandage.

I am already forty-five years old, so I think it is safe to say that this slow-growing horn I have sprouted is unlikely to be a secondary sexual characteristic. Some theories say that horns are like wisdom teeth, atavistic features we have inherited from our ancestors. My wisdom teeth grew in before I was twenty, and according to my dentist they were much bigger and harder than most. They made my mouth so swollen and sore I had to be injected with painkillers. But in the end all four of the stupid things became infected, abscessed, and eventually had to be extracted. My single secretly burgeoning little horn, on the other hand, may look meager and unimpressive, but compared to those wisdom teeth, it is vastly superior and far more useful.

Think of horns, think of demons.

Think of demons, think of magic powers!

Blow, wind, blow! If I whisper those words in a soft voice, the still air will begin to stir and a faint breeze caress my cheek. While the breeze is blowing, my horn itches like crazy. If I concentrate hard and try to cook up a really strong wind, the area around my horn tingles and I suffer such a massive headache I feel like throwing up. My horn may have practical application, but it clearly needs some fine-tuning.

Wind, stop! At my softly whispered command, the wind will cease. Of course, it could just be coincidence. The wind blows and stops on its own all the time.

Every evening after returning home from work, I scrutinize myself in a mirror. Not in a mirror large enough to show my whole face, but in a small hand mirror which I hold up to my forehead. Everyday I look at it and everyday I say the same thing:

"If this isn't a horn, I don't know what is!" I can see that my horn is gradually getting bigger, not so much in width but definitely in length. With each incremental increase, I can't help but think there will be a corresponding rise in my magical powers. I am excited by this prospect but also scared.

I went to a stationary shop and purchased a pair of drafting compasses and a clear plastic ruler. In a notebook I began recording the dimensions of my horn. After carefully positioning the sharp points of the compasses on either side of the horn and along its length, I am able to measure diameter and extension by laying the opened arms of the compasses flat against the ruler. By the end of this delicate procedure, however, I am usually dizzy from rolling my eyes upwards for so long and my hands start to shake.

What only a month ago was a tiny bump no bigger than a sesame seed, has already grown three times in size. It's three millimeters in diameter at its base, the broadest part, and almost five millimeters long. It looks for all the world as if someone has stuck a rose thorn smack in the middle of my forehead.

My horn is equidistant between my eyebrows, about two centimeters above the brow line, and it sticks straight out from my forehead. It's a shade darker than the rest of my skin, and its color actually changes subtly depending on the angle from which it is viewed. It tapers to a pointed tip which, if pressed lightly with my finger, feels soft and rubbery. It's very elastic and slowly returns to its original shape when released. While the tip is remarkably flexible, the thick base of my horn is hard and solid in the center. If I push my finger on the base deep enough, I come into contact with this hard core and it hurts a little. Not a lot, just a little. The kind of irritation you feel if you press a tiny pebble into your skin. The pain doesn't come from inside the horn itself but from pushing on something hard that is embedded in soft flesh. But the worst pain is not from putting external pressure on the horn—it's the excruciating headaches that are triggered when I try to concentrate. At those times, the soft tip of the horn is also sensitive to pain. If it's plucked, pulled or scratched, it hurts like hell.

It's not a good idea to wiggle or poke my horn too much. It gets red and inflamed and burns a little. Not only that, my brain seems to go a bit haywire. My head feels all tight and fuzzy, as if I were looking in a fogged-up mirror. Clearly my horn is no ordinary growth, it's more like a kind of antenna.

Until now my horn hasn't been very conspicuous and could pass for a wart or a mole, but recently it has begun to look more "horn-like." Being on my forehead, it's hard to miss. Sure enough one morning after staring at my forehead for a long time, a young man at work blurted out, "You've got a horn!" Everyone in the office rushed over for a look.

I work for the Botanical Information Center in one of the municipal parks. Early mornings are especially slow as there are few visitors, and there's not much to do except shoot the breeze. My co-workers formed a circle around me and were only too eager to exchange opinions.

"What an awful thing to say, calling it a horn."

"It's a wart."

"No, I think it's a pimple."

"Sure looks like a horn to me."

No one is surprised in the least that I have a horn. I know this because—well, this is the mysterious part—I seem to know exactly what each of my colleagues is thinking. I should explain that I'm not one of those people who is ultra-sensitive to the moods of others or always worried about what others are thinking. Quite frankly I don't give a fig. So this has to be my horn's doing. It seems to be picking up signals from the people around me. While my colleagues amuse themselves at my expense, my horn quivers madly, tickling my forehead mercilessly.

As soon as someone speaks, I have access to their innermost true thoughts. For instance, the man who initially spotted my horn clearly resents the fuss he's caused. What's wrong with everyone? Of course it can't be a real horn. Why are they paying so much attention to an old lady?

Someone else thinks, Big deal. The world's full of freaks.

The secretary gazes at my forehead. I've always thought she was creepy. Now she's got that horn. I hope I never end up like her. Aloud the same secretary says with great concern, "Doesn't it hurt?"

"No, not unless someone stares at it too long." I demonstrate by grimacing and pretending to press hard on my forehead. The secretary winces and backs away.

The only person who seems to feel any concern for me is my middle-aged boss, the Center Head, who lost his wife to cancer last year. Shouldn't she go to the hospital? I don't want her to feel bad so maybe it's better not to say anything, but what if it's a tumor? He returns to his desk and shouts, "Okay, everyone, back to work."

Just then a tiny voice pipes up. "People can grow horns. Don't you know that?"

It's a little girl, about five or six years old, who is looking at picture books of plants in our library corner. "I saw a boy on television with two big horns growing out of his head. They were real horns, not silly-looking things like that woman's."

The little girl speaks with such authority everyone immediately stops talking and exchanges glances. Then they start up again. Someone says he knows the program. It features freaks like a supergirl strong enough to crush a giant oil drum with a tap of her foot or a man with psychokinetic powers who can make clouds disappear at will. The boy with the horns appeared on that program. Horns are usually concealed by hair but this boy's horns sprouted just above his ears and were as thick as thumbs. Someone else says he also saw the program and that the horns were two centimeters long. Soon they are arguing about details, another person insisting the horns were five centimeters long.

Needless to say, my own horn pales in comparison and ceases to be of any interest. The general consensus is that unless your horn can shoot laser rays, you don't stand a chance of getting on that television program. The world is full of freaks, so what's a horn or two. It's nothing to brag about.

"You shouldn't believe everything you see on television," the little girl mutters under her breath.

My co-workers go back to work and when I next look around the little girl has vanished. I wish I could go after her, but I can't very well leave my desk.

I sit at the Information Desk and my job is to deal with customer inquiries and complaints. On any given day, I handle anywhere from a handful to several dozen queries all by myself. I'm the only one formally assigned to this specific function, and my colleagues have other clerical, managerial, or operational duties to attend to.

The Botanical Information Center is in the middle of a large park which also houses an art museum, a library and even tennis courts, and we are responsible for the management and maintenance of all vegetation—trees, flowers, shrubs and bushes—in the entire facility. I was transferred here and assumed my current position five years ago when the park first opened. Prior to that, I worked in the local city ward office in the department dealing with parks and roads landscaping.

I never stop to question whether I like my work or not. I just do my job, as well as I can, as diligently as I can. That's the way I am—I'm a hard worker. But ever since my horn appeared, things at work have gotten a bit out of hand.

As soon as a patron approaches my desk and begins to talk, I feel a mild jolt of electricity in my horn and before I know it, I am aware of what the person is thinking. It seems that the patron also becomes aware of something strange. Usually what happens next is that in the middle of talking the patron suddenly erupts as if he or she has lost all control, getting angry at me or letting off steam about some personal matter that has been seething inside them. Needless to say, it's not easy to work under these conditions. Of course it's my job to calm people down, and I'm good at it, more so than ever because I can now see inside them, but dealing with the raw emotions of strangers is very draining. Anyone who goes to the trouble of coming in person to complain is usually boiling with frustration and malcontent. It doesn't take much to set them off.

The Center Head notices the increase in complaints, no doubt because so many of the patrons are shouting and even getting threatening. He's probably afraid.

"There's no cause for concern, Sir," I assure him. "If the number of complaints has increased, that's proof our user numbers are up."

However, the amount of time I have to spend with each patron has also increased because they will not leave until they've gotten everything off their chest. My co-workers, on the other hand, now avoid me. If they have something to tell me, they are brief and to the point. When I can read their minds, they probably have the uncomfortable feeling of being exposed in some way. I try to exercise caution but a state of solitude seems inevitable.

The glass doors of the Center slide open and a middle-aged

woman walks in. She casts her gaze around briefly but as soon as her eyes lock on me, she marches right over.

"Excuse me, I have a question."

I give her my best public service smile. "How can I help you?"

"It's this." She holds a leaf by the tips of her fingers and waves it in front of me.

I don't have to ask, I know what this is about. Several people have already been in about the same thing. What the woman has is a leaf from the evergreen witch hazel—there is a small grove of those trees on the park grounds. On the underside of the green leaf is a smooth glossy red swelling that looks like a beautiful berry but which I know is a gall.

"Do you know what this is?" the woman demands.

"Evergreen witch hazel."

"Witch hazel?"

"That's the name of the tree your leaf comes from," I say.

"It looks beautiful, doesn't it, this shiny red fruit on the leaf. So beautiful I took it home. Well, I found out just what kind of fruit it was when I cut it open with a knife. Can you imagine my shock when hundreds of bugs came out. What the hell is that!"

"It's the type of leaf." I go over to the reference shelf and bring back a couple of books. I show her pictures of insect galls, and explain that galls can be found on many tree branches and leaves. Aphids are particularly partial to the evergreen witch hazel, which is pretty much guaranteed to have galls. Aphids just love them.

"Would you call this relationship 'symbiotic' or 'parasistic?'"

I glance at the woman's face. She looks like she is about to explode.

"Does the tree get anything out of this relationship?" she continues.

"Probably not."

"I see. So it's strictly one-way parasitic exploitation."

"Yes, I suppose you could say so."

"Yet this leaf with its nest of aphids is glossy and looks like the picture of health. Doesn't that strike you as strange?"

"Well, maybe ... " I try to be as noncommittal as possible.

"Darn right!" The woman suddenly erupts in a shrill voice. "No matter how you look at it, there's something wrong. Why don't you fumigate! I got this leaf from a public park. Do you think it's appropriate that the trees in a publicly funded park should be infested with bugs? All the plants on my veranda are now infested. It's a health hazard. What are you going to do about it!"

It's like the woman is possessed. She can't stop talking and goes from one complaint to another. Maybe under normal circumstances she is a reasonable, logical person, but at this moment it is clear she won't be able to stop until she's said everything on her mind and more. I stop listening and only catch half of what she says.

She pounces on me right away. "You! You're not paying attention!"

"Yes, I am. I'm all ears and taking notes so I can make a full report to my supervisor. That's my job."

"Is that so. A report, eh. Okay, I'll give you more to put in your report. Do you think you can just plant trees anywhere you like and leave it at that? For instance, all the trees you've planted along the roads and sidewalks. Nobody ever comes to sweep up the dead leaves. The same goes for pruning and fumigating. And don't give me that line about being short-staffed. I've heard all that."

But by the end of her tirade the woman has calmed down and in fact leaves the Center quite refreshed.

The woman just wanted someone to talk to and, in particular, to listen to her gripes. Certainly she is not alone. Every single day people come in to talk to me, bringing their grievances, their anger, their loneliness. There is a limit to anyone's patience— and by nature I am not a magnanimous person—but day after day I find I am able to listen and even give everyone a friendly smile. Surely this is all the doing of my horn.

The patrons who come to my desk with queries and complaints rarely look me in the eye. Naturally I am curious to know how people react to my horn, so I observe them carefully, but it seems that after their first glance, they do their best to ignore it. Then gradually, as if they start to get distracted, their tone softens. I want to believe that my horn has the power to expand the reality of others, to draw out their frustrations and anger, and then to erase them. I never showed any interest in strangers, but now I can't wait to see them. Such is the influence of my horn.

I wish my horn would show me only the good side of these strangers. It seems to me that would be more pleasant to observe. But when people think they're among total strangers, they don't bother putting on an act. Think about the way people look or behave when they assume no one is watching. That stupid, fed-up expression you see on so many faces, or the way people sneer contemptuously at others. How about the arrogance of people when they push their way through a crowd, glaring blue murder at anyone who gets in their way. Yet when that same person meets her friend on the street, she suddenly puts on her "good person" face. It's not a mask, it's a total metamorphosis.

I can only think of one thing that might have caused my horn to grow. About a month ago a man collided with me head on and smashed my forehead quite hard. This happened one night when I was out for a walk.

I'm in the habit of taking a stroll every night just before going to bed. Although my place of work is in the middle of a big park, I have little opportunity to stretch my legs. During the day I'm chained to my desk for long hours and by night I really need some exercise. By "night" I'm not talking about an indecently late hour. I usually go out between nine and ten o'clock, a time when there is not much traffic. I walk briskly through different parts of my neighborhood, preferring the dark alleyways to the well-lit main roads. When I return home, I only turn on a few lights so I can prolong the mood, and I take my bath and eat my dinner in the faint glow cast by the weakest setting of my fluorescent lamp. I've never been fond of lighting up the whole house like a beacon, and living by myself for so long, it's become a habit. I've often heard that single people are supposed to find coming home to a dark house unbearably lonely. But that's not the case with me. I like the dark, it's more relaxing. I have single friends who say that as soon as they get home, they walk around the house turning on all the lights. To me that's like living in a glass house, I wouldn't feel comfortable at all. But when I think about my behavior, I have to wonder if I wasn't already turning into a horned demon long ago.

I live in the house built by my grandparents, an old wooden bungalow of the type that has almost disappeared from my neighborhood. My grandparents and my parents died relatively young, leaving me to live alone in this house by the time I was in my late twenties. It's a small house with only two rooms, a kitchen and a bath. As I rarely open the wooden rain shutters and usually keep the lighting so dim, many people in the neighborhood assume the house is vacant. Surrounded on all sides by office buildings, a factory and even a twelve-story apartment building, the house is nicely sheltered and protected from probing eyes.

When I was younger I wanted to get rid of the house and move into a condominium. But the tiny plot of land on which the house stands—barely ten *tsubo*—is at the end of a narrow alley and tightly ringed by tall buildings. Fire regulations would never permit a new owner to tear down the existing structure and build a new house on the same site. Even if I wanted to sell, I could never find a buyer. My lot in life, it appears, is to live in this house until it falls apart or I die, whichever comes first. As I have no children to leave the house to, it's fitting that the house and I should rot together.

Alone in the house, I think about having to live out the rest of my days here and I feel at times like I'm already inside my own coffin buried in the earth. At times the feeling of loneliness is so overwhelming I'm at my wit's end.

Sometimes drunks stand in the shadow of the factory wall abutting my house in order to relieve themselves. It's always a shock to me, but it seems that it's the drunks who are given the real fright when they see me emerge from the darkness. "Wh ... What the hell ..." The stunned man will be riveted to the spot, his fly wide open. Really, what am I supposed to do? Then as soon as he recovers, the man usually makes a mean remark like, "Only an old hag!" as if to get back at me for scaring him.

The evening in question I'd had just such an encounter on leaving the house and it put me in a wretched mood. Earlier in the day, too, something had happened at work that really got me down, so I was doubly in the dumps.

This area is a mix of small factories and residential structures, so it's very quiet at night. The main shopping districts are far away and, unusual for Tokyo, after nine in the evening the neighborhood is almost desolate and the sound of traffic can be heard only in the distance. During the daytime there are so many cars tightly parked along the roadside that they squeeze up against the train tracks, but by this time of night, the cars are gone and it is much easier to walk on the road. Although I was born and raised amidst the dense traffic of a Tokyo neighborhood, I'm afraid of cars. I always wait for the traffic to die down before venturing out.

I trudged dejectedly along a dark road. The sky was filled with leaden clouds and the wet southerly wind carried with it a ripe stench from the sewage ditch.

This afternoon a fat old man stinking of sake marched into our Center and held me hostage for two hours while he ranted and raved. Clutching a sake bottle in one hand, he announced that his wife had divorced him as soon as he retired. He launched into a detailed account, and when he reached the end of his story, he started all over again until finally the crux of the matter emerged. He wanted the park to take all the plants and shrubs in his garden that had been left untended since his wife's departure. As the shrubs and plants had been grown from cuttings originally obtained from this park, the park should do something.

"They're my wife's bushes. I can't take care of them. I can't even take care of myself never mind bushes. They're going to get diseased and die. I feel sorry for these plants, that's why I'm here."

Several times a year cuttings from plants in the park are made available to the public for free. Over the course of ten years, this man's wife had filled her entire garden with our plants. Alternating between threats and tears, the old man showed no sign of ending his tirade.

"Women are awful. I was really betrayed. I never once saw it coming. Thirty years of living together and my wife never uttered a word of complaint or dissatisfaction. Now I'm all alone. Can't cook so I drink. Eat a bit of tofu from time to time, but basically get all my nutrients from sake. Cooking? I'll never be able to do that. Never once tried. I can't figure out why the old lady ran off like that. Men can never understand what goes on in a woman's head. Since my wife deserted me, I've been by myself. There's not enough nourishment in sake to keep a body going, though, so I know my days are numbered. But before I die, I want to do something for those plants. Any price will do. If you could just buy back those plants from me, then I could have a decent meal and put a little strength into this body."

For thirty years his wife had despised him, but the man had had no inkling. It hadn't occurred to him to wonder what went through his wife's mind day in and day out. I spent several minutes explaining carefully why it was not possible for us to buy his plants, after which the man launched into another long lament that he continued right up until closing time. At the end he burst into tears and said that unless I bought his plants, he wouldn't have any money for sake and he would die.

I walked slowly towards the river. I wanted to walk faster but there was a young couple in front of me who looked like they were returning from the public bath. Their bodies were locked together and trying to pass them would have been awkward. Although the woman did not seem pleased, the man held her hip in such a tight embrace their legs were on the verge of getting entangled. In what looked like an effort to win the woman's favor, the man was whispering something in her ear, but the woman held her head turned stiffly away and did not reply. I followed behind, maintaining a reasonable distance. As I watched the couple in front of me, I couldn't help thinking of the old man I had seen earlier and his wife. Although it was none of my business, it was clear to me that this young woman was going to leave her boyfriend soon.

While I was lost in this thought, the couple turned down a dark path running beside the ditch and suddenly vanished from sight. At the end of that path I knew there was a cluster of apartments converted from former factories and storehouses. I assumed that they rented a room there. Once back in their room, I knew they would begin arguing. It would not be a pleasant night.

I headed towards the bridge, which was still some distance off. I wanted to see the river. Whenever my nerves are on edge, I like to gaze at the streetlights reflected in the water or at the stone dike along the river bank, letting the breeze wash over me. It has a calming effect. Small animals make their homes in the stone dike, like the mice who peek out from inside the drainage pipes.

I was just about to cross the bridge when something hit me in the face with a violent impact. I distinctly remember the peculiar sensation I felt the instant I was struck. Like I was no longer human but a pure physical mass sailing through the sky. Everything was over in a split second, so fast that there was no time for any emotions to register. In the instant before I lost consciousness, a kaleidoscope of disjointed thoughts flashed through my head. Had I hit something or had someone hit me? Was it deliberate or an accident? A few days ago the sake shop daughter had been stabbed late at night by a man who had waited for her at the apartment building near my house. She'd been badly cut up. The heavy blow to my face was not a knife wound, that much I knew. Not something sharp, but something large and blunt. It was like a giant boulder had suddenly rolled across my path but I didn't have enough warning to sidestep it. It was that kind of feeling. How could I have been paying so little attention that I didn't see what was coming straight at me?

When I came to seconds later, it was just in time to see the back of a man's white shirt and to hear the light clicking sound of his footsteps retreating into the distance. Then the man was gone. That's all I saw. My head, my whole sense of awareness, felt numb, and I couldn't even ascertain what state I was in. Panicking, I entertained wild visions of myself lying in a pool of blood. In my own mind I decided that the man I saw running away must have been the young man I'd seen earlier. After having a fight with his girlfriend, he'd run out of their apartment filled with fury. When he turned onto the main road I was inadvertently blocking his path so he smashed straight into me and sent me flying. Of course, a mild concussion may have caused me to hallucinate.

Maybe the man was watching me as I lay on the ground, waiting to see if I moved, if I was alive. Then he'd know it was okay to leave. The faint scent of cigarette smoke drifted my way and I realized he must have been smoking. The only light cast was at the foot of the bridge where the mercury-vapor lamps glowed dimly.

"Are you all right?" A young man who smelled of machine oil looked at me sympathetically. I was still sitting on the ground. "What an awful man."

"You saw him?"

"He charged out of that side street, knocked you down and then ran off. Maybe I should have run after him. I was going to, but I was sure he'd just deny everything. And he looked like a pretty strong guy. I was hiding behind that electrical pole. I wasn't sure if I should call an ambulance."

He helped me stand up and I tried walking a few steps.

"Are you okay?"

"I think so."

"You've got some blood on your forehead."

I dabbed my forehead with my handkerchief. It was hard to see in the dark but there were faint streaks of blood on the cloth. I thanked the young man and asked for his name and address—I wanted to send him a small present for his help—but he politely declined so I gave him my workplace address. He didn't know the Botanical Information Center but he knew the park.

"Maybe I'll drop by sometime," he said. "I work in the watch factory over there."

My head began to buzz and inside my throbbing skull I saw a clear image of him at work, even though I'd never seen his factory before in my life. I suddenly understood other things, too. I knew that his girlfriend had rejected him, and that he wanted someone to feel sorry for him. It was embarrassing. I felt I might still be hallucinating, and I was scared.

"Please do. At least let me treat you to lunch to repay your kindness."

"It's nothing. Are you sure you're okay by yourself? Should I walk you home?"

I declined. Although it would have been nice, I also knew that despite his words, he really didn't want to.

When I touched my forehead, it felt like there was a hollow spot.

As soon as I got home, I took stock of myself. My clothes were filthy, my arms and legs scraped and cut, and there was blood everywhere. Holding up the hand mirror I kept in the bathroom, I examined my forehead. The blood had stopped but the area around the wound had turned black and blue, and indeed, my forehead was slightly indented. While I was washing the blood off my handkerchief, I developed a throbbing headache. I went to bed early but woke in the middle of the night from a nightmare. I had fallen into the river and was drowning. I thrashed my limbs desperately in the water, and the next thing I knew my body was coated not in water but in blood. I woke screaming in terror, my neck drenched in sweat, and as I wiped the sweat away with my hands I couldn't stop thinking it was blood.

When I checked in the mirror the following morning, the spot was no longer indented but raised. The middle of my forehead had swollen and a bump, like a mole, had formed. I still had my headache, although it was more of a needles and pins sensation, and I felt awful. I pulled my bangs down over my forehead to cover the swelling and went to work, where, fortunately, no one noticed a thing.

As the days passed, the swelling went down and the black discoloration faded, leaving in its place a small pointed bump. After a few more days, the bump, though still very small, began to take on the distinct shape of a little horn. My headache refused to go away, so I thought it best to see a doctor and have an X-ray taken. The doctor's explanation was that the impact of the blow I received had traumatized the surface cells of the skin, causing them to deteriorate and change form. When I asked if it would go back to normal, he gave me a noncommittal reply about how the skin tends to get bumpy with age anyway but as I wasn't that old yet maybe it would get better.

"I feel that something has changed. I don't feel right," I said.

"I see. Just what is it that has changed?"

"I don't know. My head feels tingly. It doesn't feel like my own head."

I assumed the doctor would consider sending me to one of the big hospitals for tests, but instead he just laughed.

"It's nothing. If you're worried, come back and see me in a couple of days."

Out of nowhere it suddenly came to me that the doctor was thinking about his wife and whether he should divorce her. He'd been thinking about this for the past several days. No wonder he appeared distracted. Oh, I was sick alright. The disease I had contracted was seeing things I didn't want to!

In preparation for replanting in the park, all the flowerbeds are being dug up, and maintenance staff have piled a huge mound of discarded Marguerite daisies in front of the Center. There are several thousand flowers, their roots still intact and covered with soil, forming a pile almost as tall as a child. All the daisies face the same direction, and in the hot sun, the soil around their roots as well as their leaves and stems are starting to dry out. Inside the building, we can smell the distinct sharp odor plants give off when they are damaged.

From my desk facing the glass entrance doors, I watch all morning as the mound gets smaller and smaller. There is a sign beside the daisies saying they are free for the taking, and visitors to the park carry off armfuls. Although the daisies are discards they are perfectly good. Most are in full bloom, and many have buds which have yet to open.

During the morning, it is mostly people who happen to visit the park who pick up the daisies, but by noon word has spread and local residents begin appearing in twos and threes with large bags in which they collect as many flowers as they can carry. Some even come by bicycle. The flowers disappear quickly and by early afternoon the mound is half its original size.

The witch hazel woman also shows up in the afternoon. She makes a point of coming inside the Center and confirming with me that it is okay to take the daisies. There is no trace of the threatening countenance of before—today she is all smiles. After filling the two bags she has brought with her, she leaves.

"Might be aphids in those daisies," I feel like telling her but decide in the end to forget it.

In the late afternoon the little girl also shows up, the one who declared in front of everyone that people could grow horns. She pauses in front of the mound of flowers before coming inside and then heads straight for the library corner where she pulls out an illustrated book of plants. But she keeps fidgeting and looking over at me as if my presence bothers her. I pick up a bag and go over to her side.

"If you want some flowers, you can take as many as you want," I say smiling. "Here's a bag you can use." I point to the mound of daisies outside the entrance.

At first the girl looks surprised, then she stares at me hard with her clear, intelligent-looking eyes.

"I hate flowers. They're covered with dirt and bugs, they're filthy," she says rejecting my overture in no uncertain terms. She goes back to her illustrated book of plants.

"Are you looking for something?" I ask.

"I'm just killing time."

"What kind of plants do you like?" This time not a single thought or image was coming to me from her. I feel panic-stricken.

"None in particular."

"But you're studying that book so intently."

I can tell my persistence is annoying her. When I try to peer over her shoulder to see what she is looking at, the girl quickly leans forward to cover the page.

"I'm just looking," she says curtly.

It makes me mad being ignored, so I bend down close to her ear and whisper, "Did you know that people with horns have the power to make any wish come true?"

At last the girl lifts her head from her book and looks me straight in the eye. Those lovely round opaque eyes stare right inside me and in that instant I feel inexplicably nervous. I feel as if everything is visible to this girl, that she knows all the worst things about me.

The girl looks at me suspiciously and shakes her head. "I don't believe you."

Why am I so uptight about winning this little girl over? My heart is beating loudly.

"Okay, maybe granting wishes sounds funny," I continue pompously. "It's better to say I can read other people's minds." What on earth is making me brag like that? I hate myself.

The girl is quick on the draw. "Then tell me why I come here to look at this book. If you can answer that correctly, I'll believe you."

I'm stumped.

"See," the girl says triumphantly, "you're lying. People don't have horns. How dumb can you be."

After the girl leaves, I feel thoroughly depressed and certainly not in the mood to do any work. Why did she come here to look at that book? I have absolutely no idea. I spend the rest of the day watching women collect daisies outside. There are housewives, working women, students. One by one I think I can see into their lives and their personalities but whether I am right or not, I have no way of checking.

As I watch the women swarm around the mound of flowers shamelessly trying to grab as many as they can hold, I repeat the little girl's words. "I hate flowers." In my empty head, two scenes appear of the little girl when she is older—one a rape scene and the other of her failing her entrance exams. But I know immediately these scenes come from inside me—they are my emotions and have nothing to do with her. I'm losing my confidence. I am nothing but a loathsome human being.

Just before dusk, groups of women returning from work rush into the park and take the last of the flowers. Some men on their way home stop to observe the scene of swarming women from afar. After everyone is gone, all that remains are some wilted leaves fluttering on a pile of dirt.

I recall the young man who smelled of machine oil. He has a girlfriend, my instinct tells me, and although he may be disappointed many times in love eventually he will meet the right woman. He is young, he has a chance. He's not like me, someone who will probably go through her entire life without love. We aren't even part of the same species.

Initially I feel so certain he will show up any day at the Botanical Center with his girlfriend that I can't take my eyes off the glass doors. But my instinct seems to be failing. The days pass, and he hasn't come. In the meantime all the flowerbeds have been replanted, and a pale purple flower is in bloom. The little girl has stopped coming too. I would like to apologize if I ever see her again.

My mind and my horn are gradually moving in a strange, perverse direction. My forehead is in pain all the time and my poor little horn is starting to shrivel up. It droops now, and has lost its shape.

But worst, I'm plagued by nightmares. An old boyfriend appears every night and pleads with me, but I can't catch what he's saying. He loses his temper, swears at me. Then as soon as I wake up, I remember that I never had a real relationship with him. I dreamt of him because at one point I'd had a crush on him. Another night I dream of the large man who knocked me down; I dream that he is hit by a car and suffers gruesome injuries. In my dreams I wish for terrible things to happen to others. Can it be that my puny, stunted horn nurtures only the most puny, stunted delusions?

One day I open the newspaper and see a tiny article tucked away in the corner—a murder in the new apartment building by the river, the one erected on the site of a former factory. The victim is a twenty-one year-old bargirl, and the murder suspect is her twenty-six year-old unemployed boyfriend with whom she was living. He has gone missing. As soon as I read the article, I know for sure it is the couple I saw. The fact is they just appeared in my dream last night, conducting a violent argument inside my head.

What if my dreams are prophetic? What should I do? Sleep brings me no rest and I can't help but feel a deep foreboding.

∾

Mirror

The first thing Ichiko saw was the woman's face. Floating in the water, a blur. That was why she thought she must be in the water, that was why she thought she was about to die. It troubled her that she was dying, but it troubled her just as much that she didn't know who the woman was. With the woman floating right in front of her, she couldn't die properly. Then, in the midst of all this distress, Ichiko remembered a television program she had seen years ago and the legend of the Amazon otter came rushing to mind.

On clear nights when the full moon shone brightly, legend had it that the otter who lived in the Amazon River turned into a beautiful woman and waited by the riverbank to seduce men. Ichiko had never been able to forget the old Brazilian man who claimed he had met one of these creatures. He looked ferocious and his skin was burnt black by the sun, but he had worn a puckish grin on his face as he told his tale.

"I guess I can tell you now because it happened so long ago. It was different then. Back in those days, otters lived in this region. It was right after the birth of our first child, when my wife was still recovering from childbirth, the umbilical cord barely cut. I went to the river to draw water. It was autumn and the sun set early. Just as I was about to return home, I looked up and saw a beautiful woman standing beside the riverbank. In my entire life, I have never seen a more ravishing beauty. I was completely spellbound. Of course, I knew right away she was the otter woman.

"She beckoned me with her hand, come hither, come hither. Well, I was sorely tempted, believe me. But my wife and baby were asleep at home waiting for me to make supper and I was very hungry, so I went straight home. I always wondered what became of that beauty but no matter how many times I went back to the river, I never saw her again. I wish she would come back and invite me again. I'd follow her in an instant. I'm done with making dinners for the wife and family."

The old man had faced the television camera head on, winked and waved his hand to demonstrate how the otter woman had beckoned him. Come hither, come hither. Being a foreigner it was hard for Ichiko to tell his exact age, but she guessed he was at least seventy.

The creature floating in front of Ichiko was definitely not the otter woman of the Amazon legend, of that she was certain. This woman was neither attractive nor did she beckon with her hand. She had big bulging eyes and wore a totally blank expression. Just as Ichiko was wondering what the woman might do, the face suddenly turned into the head of a very large fish. The fish glared at Ichiko through the dark water. Instinctively, she glared back.

It seemed to her that these thoughts must have come in fragments that poked through the murky haze of her consciousness. She couldn't have remembered the old man's story in one fell swoop. It was only an illusion of smooth recollection, caused by a reflex instinct to string together the unconnected shards of memory that flickered across her brain. Seeing the woman's face could not have been real, and as for it turning into a fish, that was downright peculiar. The fact that Ichiko hadn't thought it peculiar at the time was definitely a sign that her head wasn't right. Of course, when you believe you are dying, nothing you think of can really be said to be strange.

She learned afterwards that she hadn't fallen into the river at all. Instead it appeared she'd fallen off the other side of the high cliff-like embankment, hit her head on the hard ground and lost consciousness. That was when she realized that one's mind and memory were totally unreliable, capable of making up utter nonsense. It left her with a queasy feeling. Although she assumed she had been unconscious the whole time, in fact she had drifted in and out of consciousness, even getting up, walking around and speaking. She heard this from others, but because she had no memory of it herself, she couldn't believe it. If she were going to die, then she didn't mind, but as long as her consciousness hung on, it appeared her life refused to end.

Between the time she fell and the time she regained consciousness, she hadn't experienced any fear. That gave her some courage. The doctor who attended to her injuries was cut and dry. "Don't worry, you'll live. In a month, you'll be up and walking again."

Yet she couldn't remember a single thing about the accident. At one point before she understood what had happened, it seemed she had yelled repeatedly, "I'm dying, I'm dying." It was all quite mortifying. She had a crystal clear recollection of the moment just before the accident, right down to the shape of the plants growing on the side of the path, but the fact that she couldn't remember anything after that was very frustrating. It could have happened yesterday, the day before yesterday, or much longer ago. She simply didn't know.

The accident occurred while she was riding her bicycle home from work. Everyday she rode the same familiar narrow path on the embankment beside the river. The dirt path was poorly lit, the lamps dim and positioned far apart. It was a windless night, the air veiled with a light mist that seemed to concentrate the glow around the lamps, leaving the surrounding areas in shadow. As Ichiko propelled her bicycle slowly forward through the dim light, she felt her own faint shadow fade into the darkness. Under the bright light of day, the water in the river was brackish and muddy, but at this time of the evening the river looked lovely, wrapped in the pale darkness with the lights of the buildings on the opposite bank reflected in its water. Although the buildings themselves were ugly, when reflected in the water they were transformed into a dazzling show of lights. Somehow when the dirty buildings and the dirty water were put together, they turned into a thing of beauty. Ichiko stopped her bicycle to admire the view.

The buildings were upside-down towers of light whose hard concrete edges dissolved in the water, giving them a fragile appearance. The lights burned brightly in the water as if they were released from the buildings, free to swim on their own in the river. Whenever she looked at the river at this time of evening, Ichiko always had the same thought—the best way to die would be to throw herself into this night river. To be clothed in those lights, to be reborn as a small luminous fish, to claim for herself the length and breadth of the entire river, what a delicious feeling that would be. She didn't have to worry about people swimming in the river, she could have it all to herself. And if she were dying, it didn't matter that the river was a bit polluted.

On days when it rained, however, the water got churned up and the river gave off a foul odor. It didn't seem like such a nice place to die then. On rainy days, Ichiko avoided this route.

To enjoy the lights, she got off her bicycle and squatted by the river's edge. The silent black water reflected her feelings like a mirror. When she looked at the river, she understood things about herself. Inside her own heart was a river much deeper, much wider, much blacker than this river. It was filled with every thought she had ever had but was never able to share with another, and by now it was so full and overflowing as to make her swoon. The river inside her had nowhere to go and the water continued to rise until lately it seemed so very heavy. Unlike the river before her which sparkled with dancing lights, her own river was dark. No light shone in.

Ichiko peered down at the surface of the night river. If she jumped into the river, would the black waters in her own body seep out into the river and would Ichiko at last begin to shine radiantly? The lights were only surface reflections, they were not part of the river itself, and yet there was beauty in the river as it reflected the lights and in the lights as they were reflected in the river. Whatever dirty sludge was at the bottom of the river was hidden from sight. The surface was all that mattered—if it looked pretty, that was enough, she thought.

Ichiko continued walking, pushing her bicycle beside her. She passed businessmen returning home, couples, joggers, some drunks. There were a number of disheveled-looking men, apparently homeless, who walked aimlessly by themselves. Some were empty-handed while others carried large shopping bags stuffed with all their worldly possessions. Brightly lit tennis courts were enclosed by a high mesh fence, and half of the people watching the couples play appeared to be vagrants. They had no place to call home. Or if they did have a home, it was a bed of thick bushes by the riverbank.

The path along the top of the embankment was crowded with people walking or riding bicycles. Most were rushing home, but there were those who would make the park their home after everyone else had left. Ichiko felt herself dissolving into the twilight scene, so inconspicuous she was virtually invisible.

People either rushed past her like shadows or else they stood perfectly still. Standing still gave one cover, it was the way the homeless remained inconspicuous. The people in a rush looked angry, each one of them wearing an expression that seemed to say he suffered more than anyone else. It seemed normal to look like this. And yet, in a matter of time—how long would it be—every one of them would be gone from the face of the earth.

The side of the embankment that faced the river was a sheer vertical drop made of concrete. The other side was also a steep slope but it was made of dirt and covered with thick brush and weeds. At points along the pathway there were stone staircases leading down to the foot of the embankment where the cherry trees were. The trees had been planted so close together their upper branches intertwined, and when they were in full bloom, the air was pink and filled with an undulant sea of blossoms. People crowded below the thick blossoms to drink and party until the sea of pink was drenched in the smell of alcohol. For flower viewing at night, mercury lamps had been installed at strategic intervals and a walkway had been created from colored flagstones arranged in a mosaic pattern. But the cherry blossoms had come and gone and the trees were now covered with a dense growth of foliage.

The embankment was about three times the height of the average person. This was the distance Ichiko fell when she went tumbling down, bicycle and all, flying through the air and crashing headlong into trees. She cracked several ribs, sprained her neck, and ended up covered head to toe in bruises. She had no recollection of what caused her fall and could not remember the crash itself. She couldn't even remember being afraid.

Apparently she was lying half-buried by the tall grasses on the slope, and her bicycle had been flung some distance away. She was taken by ambulance to hospital, rushed into emergency surgery, and then slept day and night. Someone in the hospital explained all this to her later. It was during this time that Ichiko had hallucinated about being submerged underwater. She had become a water wraith, bobbing up and down on the waves or simply staring at the water. "She's coming to," she heard someone say, at the precise moment when the face of the woman in the water changed into a fish. Waking from the general anesthetic, Ichiko assumed this was the first time she had regained consciousness, but in fact since her fall, she had drifted in and out of consciousness several times.

When the police came to the hospital to investigate the accident, the wounds inside Ichiko's mouth hurt when she talked. She managed to ask who had phoned for the ambulance.

"Didn't you dial emergency yourself?" The officer was surprised by her question. According to the record, the call had been placed by a woman. She said she had been injured, was unable to move and could someone please help her. The directions had been a bit vague but good enough.

Seeing Ichiko's perplexed look, the officer offered another suggestion. "Perhaps it was a passer-by, someone who made the call but then left the scene. Of course, that's a pretty isolated spot. Not too many people pass by there. If you'd fallen into the river, it would have been a different story. You'd have gotten everyone's attention immediately."

"I don't remember a thing," she said.

If she'd fallen into the river. When he said those words, Ichiko winced. She wished she had fallen into the river. She told the police officer and the attending physician that she couldn't recall anything, that all she could remember were her name, address and place of employment. She would have liked to conveniently "forget" her own name, too, but it was all over her belongings so there was no point in trying to hide it.

"Sometimes a strong shock can result in temporary amnesia," the doctor explained. "The patient doesn't forget everything, just certain things, the things he or she wants to forget. It's a natural protective instinct."

The officer continued. "Okay, just tell me anything you can remember about what happened. No good? All right, but if you recall something later, please contact me. If you were pushed, this is a criminal assault case. It's our duty as police to investigate."

The doctor had used the word amnesia. Ichiko decided that must be what she had, and she stopped trying to force herself to remember. If she had forgotten, it must be something she didn't want to remember and it was best to leave it forgotten. She was exhausted. As soon as the officer was finished, she felt herself drifting off. She felt like she was suffocating. She was no longer in the hospital, she was sinking into a cold place. Then, as if her head had broken through the surface of water, she could breathe again. She experienced a sense of relief but when she came to she realized her consciousness had returned in its same ambiguous form.

Ichiko thought the police officer had gone but he was still there. He and the doctor had their backs to her and were whispering about something. Was it another day or the continuation of just a few minutes ago? Was she still dreaming? She tried stealthily wriggling the tips of her fingers and toes under the blanket as a check, but they hardly moved at all.

The officer's voice sounded far away, as if it were coming from a neighboring room, yet it had a penetrating quality that echoed inside her head. Yes, yes, the doctor responded in a low voice that sounded much closer.

"Will she regain her memory?" the officer asked.

"It's hard to say."

"What are the chances she might commit suicide?"

"I don't want to think about that. The body's reaction to the strong shock of an accident can be more than loss of memory, and the patient can fall into a temporary state of depression."

"I see. It's hard to believe that after sustaining injuries that are going to keep her in hospital for a month she could have walked fifty meters to make a phone call and then returned to her original spot."

What a hateful suspicious man, Ichiko thought. The two men seemed to sense that she was listening to their conversation, for their voices suddenly dropped and she could no longer hear them.

Her awareness was like something that floated up from the bottom of the river and kept breaking off into bits. Instead of a smooth continuous thread of thought, her conscious mind was tangled in lumpy knots, and these knots of awareness were like hard balls of pain. Her whole body hurt, on the outside and on the inside. It hurt yet she couldn't really feel the pain. Perhaps her nerves had been dulled by the anesthetic, but the pain didn't feel like it belonged to her. It was someone else's pain that she was being forced to shoulder, a pain she wasn't responsible for.

The knots of pain made movement impossible. Thinking was no easier. By the time she reached the end of a thought she had forgotten the beginning. She stopped trying to think. Whatever someone said to her, she agreed with, and if no one spoke to her, she lay quietly asleep like a rag doll. The staff in the hospital were very busy, so it was rare that anyone talked to her. The police no longer came. As her head gradually became clearer, it was frustrating not to be able to remember anything, but the doctor had warned her that fretting would only slow down her recovery so she tried hard not to get upset. One of the best techniques she discovered for creating a sense of calm was to imagine herself lying at the bottom of a clear river, looking up at the water above. When she did this she felt her personality was erased and that she was returned to being a hard mass of pure existence. As she lay immobile on the river floor, she felt a sense of expectancy, as if waiting for someone to float down from above. A water wraith would float down and Ichiko would breathe life into her. That vision she had had earlier of a woman floating underwater was surely a water wraith. She must have been the one who dialed emergency. Letting these random thoughts drift through her mind was oddly soothing.

Her first recollection came to her many days later. She was riding her bicycle along the embankment admiring the city lights reflected on the still surface of the river. It was calm—the wind that had been blowing throughout the day had died down at dusk—and several stars had just emerged in the pale early evening sky. They couldn't yet compete with the brilliance of the artificial lights of the buildings reflected in the water, but Ichiko thought they would look lovely reflected in the river and she decided to wait until it got darker. Thinking she would go back and find a nice spot to wait near the bridge, she had just started to make a U-turn when a bicycle without any lights came bearing down on her.

The rider was a large, burly young man whose body swayed from side to side as he pumped his bicycle fast in an exaggerated zigzag path. In the split second when she thought for sure they would collide, Ichiko closed her eyes. Everything went black. She couldn't remember anything else.

Either he knocked her over by running into her, or by passing so close he caused her to lose her balance and fall over the side of the embankment. The man on the bicycle might not even have bothered to look back. Or if he had and noticed that the woman and her bicycle had suddenly vanished, might he not have run away in a panic?

She felt the faint stirrings of a physical memory—her body tilting to one side, the earth slipping away from under her feet, the path beneath the wheels of her bicycle disappearing. She thought she even dimly recollected the actual pain of impact, but it might have been the pain she was experiencing now. Lying in the hospital bed with nothing else to do, all manner of unconnected thoughts shot into her head. Ichiko had no way of distinguishing reality from a memory she was making up.

The doctor couldn't tell if she'd been in a direct collision or not. True, her injuries were serious—broken bones, cuts and bruises all over her body—but it was also possible that these wounds were caused by her own bicycle or from crashing hard into trees and the ground. The doctor's voice had trailed off uncertainly.

Colleagues from work visited Ichiko in the hospital, but as she wasn't particularly close to anyone, the visits were formal and brief.

"What a terrible thing to have happen," one co-worker said. "Take your time recovering. Don't worry about work."

"You were really lucky," another said. "Hurry up and get better and come back to work. We're all waiting for you."

"Good thing you didn't get it in the face," someone else said.

Yet another commented, "For heaven's sake, cheer up! You should look a bit happier."

She'd worked with these people for years, but making conversation with them outside the office felt strained. There was nothing to say.

She didn't tell anyone else. She didn't feel like seeing anyone. As the doctor had said, probably she was depressed. She didn't want to talk, and the thought of having to listen to someone else's chatter was equally unappealing. But she didn't mind it when the nurses or the nursing assistants talked to her or touched her. It occurred to her that maybe she liked women better than men.

She thought about the otter woman in the Amazon over and over, especially the part where the old man said he was ready to go with her if asked again. Ichiko found that part grating. She knew that after the first time, the otter woman had given up on him. There was no second chance.

How beautiful would the otter woman have been? Ichiko thought about the most beautiful women she had ever known and tried to imagine someone even more beautiful, more perfect. But no image came to her, probably because she was trying to imagine someone who would appeal to the taste of the old man. When she thought about the kind of woman she would follow, suddenly the possibilities and varieties were limitless. One after the other, images of striking women filled her mind. She could spend the whole day fantasizing about them.

By rights she should have been thinking about handsome men, but Ichiko was quite certain she had no interest in running off with a man.

So far no one in Ichiko's life had ever proposed to her, although someone had once gone as far as saying, "If I were to do it again, I'd marry you." The man was a colleague at work, and to this day they continued to work in the same office. At the time when he spoke those words, though, he was a newlywed, someone who Ichiko on a lark had invited back to her apartment one evening after work.

"Just married and doing something like this ... I'm a terrible human being," he said as he tore off his clothes.

Afterwards, he made no move to leave and gave the impression that he intended to stay over. Then, suddenly in the middle of the night, he leapt up and began getting dressed.

"You're not staying?" Ichiko asked.

"Once before I stayed out all night and my wife really blew her stack. I never thought she'd get so angry." By the look on his face, this was not a made-up excuse. "You know, if I'd met you first, I'm sure I would have married you. Too bad about the timing. If I could get married all over again, I'd pick you. I've got to go now, but I'll come again, okay."

Ichiko swore on the spot that if she ever got married, it would definitely not be to him. The man subsequently invited himself over to her apartment many times, always leaving in the dead of night.

Soon the man became a father. Like the old man in the Brazilian forest, Ichiko imagined him rushing home every night after work to tend to the needs of his newborn baby and his housebound wife. The news of his baby's birth had reached Ichiko indirectly through the office grapevine, and sure enough whenever she ran into the man at work he would avert his eyes. Of course he stopped dropping by Ichiko's place.

Several months later, they bumped into each other in the corridor at work. No one else was around, and the man drew up close. "Been a long time. How about if I came over tonight?" He laughed nervously and put his hand on Ichiko's shoulder.

"I'd rather you didn't." Ichiko turned her face away.

The man looked at her. "What the hell's wrong?"

"I'd just rather you didn't."

"Why not?"

"Please don't come over anymore."

The man's face hardened into an angry, suspicious glare. "I see. Well, if that's the case, the feeling is mutual. I certainly don't want to be in your way. Quite frankly, I'm disgusted."

When Ichiko didn't reply, the man walked away.

She busied herself with work for the rest of the day and did her best to banish the man from her thoughts. But that night at home while she was lying in bed, a strong wind suddenly blew up outside and as she lay still listening to the noisy rattling of her windowpanes, she found herself wishing she could become one with the wind and fling herself hard against the window. The man's remarks had infuriated her. How dare he criticize her, he of all people, jumping to his own hasty conclusions that she'd found someone else. She wished she'd been able to come up with a sharp retort. It was enough to make her want to seduce him again and really turn his family life on its head. But what was the point? It wasn't love. It was simply the challenge of wanting to bag a newly married man as her trophy. The man's wife used to work for the same company, and for many years she and Ichiko sat together at adjoining desks. Ichiko had known that she was engaged but not to whom. Just before the woman quit her job, she confided in Ichiko.

"I haven't told anyone else but the man I'm going to marry is someone you know quite well. Would you like to know who it is?"

She was not a particularly attractive woman, certainly not the kind one took notice of, but at that moment her face was absolutely radiant. From that point on, Ichiko couldn't help but be conscious of the woman's fiancé and she began observing him carefully. After the woman quit the company, Ichiko made up excuses to get closer to the man.

Recalling these episodes from her past made Ichiko feel frightened about her future. She got so worked up she was unable to fall asleep and lay awake until dawn, the howling of the wind in her ears.

A few days after she was hospitalized, the man came with a group of colleagues from work to visit her. He stayed at the back of the group, looking bored and indifferent as if to say that coming here hadn't been his idea. He barely even glanced at Ichiko. When the group left, the man filed out of the hospital room with everyone else, but at the doorway he turned around. "I'll come again," he said in what seemed like a deliberately loud voice. For an instant, the expression on the man's face was the same as the old man in the Brazilian forest, the look of a man hungry for a second chance at temptation. When Ichiko's eyes locked with the man's, she thought she might feel some excitement but she felt nothing at all. It convinced her that no matter what the reason, for a woman once was enough.

It was so obvious—she'd simply been jealous of another woman's happiness. Later that same night after the man's visit, when the nurses had retreated to the nursing station and all was quiet and still on the ward, Ichiko found herself remembering the woman who had become the man's wife. Instead of the man, she wished that she had gotten to know the woman better.

Recently, very recently, Ichiko had become aware of how women excited her imagination. Men made her depressed and irritated, but when it came to women—women she knew or total strangers—she fell into a blissful trance thinking about their faces or forms. When one of the young nursing assistants gave her a sponge bath, Ichiko felt overcome by the urge to reach out and stroke her wrist or caress her nape as it peek-a-booed out of the collar of her uniform, so that before Ichiko knew it her heart was pounding furiously. It took her by complete surprise.

It didn't seem to matter who the woman was. If she caught sight of a nurse or nursing assistant, she couldn't take her eyes off her, wishing she could bring the woman closer. She wondered if her head hadn't gone funny when she hit it in her fall, but what did her head have to do with the throbbing ache her body felt when she gazed at another woman? Of all the nursing staff, Ichiko was particularly fond of Taniyama-san, one of the youngest of the nursing assistants. She was so sensitive to Ichiko's gaze that as soon as their eyes met she would immediately say, "Is anything wrong?" tilting her delicate neck in a most charming way. She was tall with pale white skin, and her whole body looked soft and supple. When Ichiko asked her to comb her hair or straighten her blanket, any little task she could think of, Taniyama-san would smile gently and do whatever she'd been asked right away. She didn't act too busy or put upon like the others. As the days passed, Ichiko found it was only Taniyama-san she hoped to see.

One day when Taniyama-san was looking even more lovely than usual, Ichiko impulsively called her over.

"I'm sorry to bother you when you're so busy, but I wonder if you could lend me a mirror."

As soon as she spoke, Ichiko knew what she wanted to do—she wanted to see the two of them side by side reflected in a mirror. Taniyama-san beamed. "A mirror! Good, that's a sign you're getting better." She quickly fished inside the pocket of her white uniform and pulled out a small compact mirror which she handed to Ichiko. Unlike all the others who smelled so medicinal, when Taniyama-san drew close Ichiko could smell the fresh scent of soap.

"Even without a mirror, Matsuzaki-san, I hope you know you're very attractive."

"Not me. The pretty one is you. See how pretty you are."

So saying, Ichiko tilted the mirror in Taniyama-san's direction and stole a sidelong glance at the reflection. In the tiny mirror, Taniyama-san's face rose like the ghostly face of the woman Ichiko had seen floating in the dark water. Her face wore a sad, slightly out of focus expression. Taniyama-san stared intently at her reflection, then broke into a smile.

"Matsuzaki-san, you're a bit of an oddball," she said. Then, as if amused by her own words, she repeated, "An oddball."

"I must have hit my head funny when I fell."

The expression on Taniyama-san's face suddenly turned very serious. "No, that's not true. I'm sorry, did it bother you that I called you that?"

"Not at all."

"People all look more or less the same on the outside, but as soon as you get to know them as individuals, you find something strange about them. That's why I'm afraid of getting close to others. I guess that makes me an oddball, too."

"Isn't it okay to be odd?"

"Is it? That's good to know. Here, keep the mirror as a token of my thanks." When Taniyama-san looked up, her eyes shone with moisture.

Ichiko didn't see her for several days in a row after that, and when she finally asked one of the other nursing assistants, she was told that Taniyama-san had quit her job.

Ichiko could not get Taniyama-san out of her mind. Why had she quit? Even as she prepared to take an electrocardiogram, Ichiko found it impossible to clear her head of the thoughts swirling inside. "You need to relax," the technician administering the test said. Ichiko worried that her head was a transparent shell, every thought plainly visible for all to see. It wouldn't do to get a funny reading on the electrocardiogram, and have her discharge from the hospital postponed.

To calm herself Ichiko again imagined she was lying flat at the bottom of the water but suddenly out of nowhere Taniyama-san's body came floating down on top of her and she became excited all over again. To push Taniyama-san from her thoughts, Ichiko forced herself to think about other women, women who were more beautiful, more alluring than Taniyama-san. Like the otter, what kind of beautiful woman would she wish to be transformed into? She tried out several models in her head. She burrowed into her fantasy world as if digging into an underwater riverbed. The watery realm of her imagination was warm and silent, the deeper she dug, the more intense were her sensations. It was a world filled with women all there for the choosing. When Ichiko began swimming towards the women, they suddenly noticed her and in unison beckoned her with their hands to come closer. Each woman looked different; her face, her figure, her hairstyle were unique. Ichiko carefully looked each one over, dressing them in flattering clothes and combing their tresses. In imitation, the women in turn did the same thing to her. Under the tender stroking hands of the women, Ichiko felt herself being reborn a younger, more beautiful woman, and she became one of them, her naked body locked in embrace with them. Absorbed in play, she forgot all time. Even in her own imagination, she wasn't sure if she was the master of these women or their slave.

As Ichiko created each new imaginary woman, a woman in the real world disappeared. It happened whenever the woman beckoned a man and he hesitated—in that instant she dissolved. All the vanished women immediately forgot about men and lived happily in their new world. At some point, Taniyama-san appeared in the midst of the group. She took off her uniform and smiled, looking more radiant than ever.

Before she knew it, Ichiko couldn't think of anything else.

Her reveries were interrupted by the screaming wail of an ambulance siren piercing the night. The patter of rapid footfalls running up and down the hospital corridor echoed inside her head and reverberated right down into her wounds. The women in Ichiko's head fell silent as if they had died. They fluttered like long strands of seaweed in the water.

The next morning the hospital halls again filled with clamor, and Ichiko wondered if it was a continuation of the commotion around last night's emergency.

One of the older nursing assistants came into Ichiko's room looking distressed. "You were close to Taniyama-san, weren't you. Did she ever say anything to you?"

Ichiko didn't reply. A feeling of foreboding came over her.

The nursing assistant lowered her voice. "She's dead. The man she was living with killed her. Can you imagine! She was so young, and she had such a sweet face. But, you know, I always thought she was a strange one. She was very guarded about her personal life. You used to talk to her a lot, didn't you. Taniyama-san seemed to be very attached to you. She was quite upset that the man who caused your accident hadn't been caught. Well, you can't tell a person's life from the outside, can you. Oh, I shouldn't be talking like this."

"Don't worry, I won't say anything."

"Thanks. I don't know why I'm so worked up. Why the hell did she have to get herself killed."

"I heard an ambulance last night. Was that her?" asked Ichiko.

"Yes, I just found out myself this morning. Imagine being brought back to the same hospital where you used to work."

"Have they caught her killer?"

"I don't think so. I thought I heard he got away, but I can try to find out."

Not long afterwards, Ichiko was discharged from hospital right on schedule, one month after being admitted. At first she feared that her recovery might take longer but the improvements in the last week were dramatic. The results of the final round of tests just before her discharge showed no sign of damage to the brain whatsoever, meaning there was little danger of lingering ill effects.

After a short period of recuperation at home, Ichiko stopped needing her cane and was soon able to go back to work. One day on her way home from the office, she decided to walk along the riverbank. Of course, she no longer had her bicycle and had to take the bus to the closest stop and walk from there, but it wasn't as tiring as she thought it might be. That unexpected keepsake, the pocket mirror, was always tucked carefully in her handbag and went with her wherever she went. She had never once looked at her own reflection in it. She wanted Taniyama-san's face to remain locked inside forever.

It was amazing how many people were out strolling on the embankment. There were a lot riding bicycles, too. If the man who had knocked her over was here, Ichiko felt confident she could pick him out by the unique way he had of pedaling. She began searching the crowd for him, but almost immediately she was distracted by the sight of a beautiful woman coming in her direction. Before she knew it, Ichiko was following her.

∽

Time

Kasumi nodded off to the loud roar of the subway. She dreamed that she was being tossed about by the wind, and when she reached her station, her head was throbbing slightly. She went through the exit turnstile and climbed the long flight of stairs to the street level, ignoring the elevator. Outside it was very windy. Sand blew in her face and dark clouds raced overhead so fast the entire sky seemed to be spinning. Patches of blue peeked out here and there behind some low-lying clouds.

The wind was cold and smelled of chlorine. It stung, and Kasumi realized the backs of her hands were covered with cuts as if an iron nail had been dragged over them. When she licked her wounds, she felt her lips were swollen too.

The area around the station was empty and had a half-finished look, as if construction work had been abandoned before completion. She was starving. At the intersection directly in front of the station, there was a motorcycle shop, shoe store, bookshop, and beauty parlor, but there didn't seem to be any place that sold food. In the distance she could make out something that looked like a red bridge. This was clearly the expressway Yamaguchi had told her to look for. He lived in the black apartment highrise just this side of the expressway, he'd said, the only tall building in the neighborhood so it was impossible to miss.

She decided to forget about getting something to eat and began walking in the direction of Yamaguchi's apartment. That was the precise moment when the maddening hot itch between her toes decided to flare up. Stupid Athlete's foot! The peeling skin between her toes was thoroughly disgusting—she'd never had anything like this before in her whole life. There was no other explanation. She must have caught it from that man.

She passed a paint shop, packing warehouse, real estate agency, and a tatami maker. On the other side of the street there was a noodle shop and seafood restaurant, but both were closed. The last store she came to was a drugstore, which a middle-aged woman with fair skin was just opening up.

Kasumi went inside and asked for a toothbrush and Athlete's foot medication.

"Any special brand?" the woman inquired.

"Something fast-working."

The woman selected a product from the shelf. "How about this one?"

After Kasumi paid for her purchases, the woman reached under the counter and brought out a box filled with small paper triangles.

"Take two," she urged.

Kasumi selected two paper triangles and gave them to the woman who snipped the ends with a pair of scissors. She unfolded the first triangle, smiled, and told Kasumi she'd just won a prize. It turned out to be a kilo of potatoes. When she left the store, Kasumi noticed the handwritten sign on the door: "Play 'Instant Lottery' and win some delicious Hokkaido potatoes!"

As soon as she went out into the cold again, her lips started to smart and she regretted not buying lip balm, but the thought of having to play "Instant Lottery" all over again was enough to keep her from going back. She continued on her way. It was that man's fault. He'd kissed her so much her lips had gone funny. Even now they still weren't normal. She'd managed to break up with him, thank goodness, so she didn't have to put up with any more of his smooching. But what was she going to do about these "mementos" he'd left her. What if the puffiness in her lips and the ringworm between her toes never got better? Kasumi ran her tongue over her chapped lips, and a small piece of skin flaked off and stuck to her tongue. As she bent over to spit it out, she noticed the woman at the drugstore was standing outside and seemed to be watching her.

Kasumi checked her watch: 9:15 A.M. She had called Yamaguchi at 7:30 to ask if she could come over, and he had told her he would leave for work at a little after 9:00. If she couldn't make it in time, maybe she should wait until the evening, he'd suggested. Kasumi had rushed over as fast as she could.

When he answered the door, Yamaguchi looked rather annoyed.

"Okay, come in. I don't know what this is about. You can spend the day here, but I have to go to work now. Whatever it is you want to talk about will have to wait till I get back."

They traded places in the cramped entranceway, Kasumi taking her shoes off and Yamaguchi putting his on.

"Do you mind if I use your kitchen?"

"Go ahead. Just be careful with the gas."

"I want to cook some potatoes. I just won a whole bagful."

"Did you get those from Ito Drugs?" Yamaguchi noticed the plastic bag Kasumi set down in the entryway. "I won some too a few days ago. They're around here somewhere. Help yourself."

Yamaguchi gave her the key and hurried off. Once she was alone, she felt so thoroughly at home in his apartment it was as if the place were hers and she'd been living here for ages. Despite being here for almost a year, Yamaguchi had hardly any furniture and the apartment still looked brand new. Everything was gleaming white, from the sparkling walls to the ceiling, from the shiny new fridge to the washing machine. Steam rose from the half-full pot of coffee on the kitchen table. Kasumi got a cup from the cupboard and helped herself. Then she washed two potatoes, put them in a pot of water and turned on the gas. Through the ventilation fan above the stove she could hear the wind howling outside. She couldn't remember if it had been this windy when she left her apartment a couple of hours ago.

As soon as the potatoes were done, she sprinkled them with salt and ate them. Then she went into the bathroom to wash her face and her feet. Running the water on her hands made the cuts smart, and she was conscious once again that she must have injured herself in this morning's scuffle.

Next she sat down on Yamaguchi's bed—it had a faint male odor—but although she wanted to take a nap, she knew she was too upset and it wasn't likely she'd be able to sleep. In her mind she went over what had happened.

In the still-dark early hours of the morning, Kasumi's former lover had showed up at her doorstep, and in a voice loud enough to wake up the entire neighborhood, had begun raising hell. That whole night he had called her on the phone but she had refused to answer. Finally, close to dawn, she took the receiver off the hook. Clearly he had been calling from a nearby pay phone, for in a matter of minutes he was pounding violently on her door.

"Kasumi! Open up! Come on out!" he screamed at the top of his lungs when she didn't answer the door.

She couldn't let him go on like that, so she quickly got dressed and yanked the door open. She caught him completely off-guard—it was the last thing he'd thought she would do. She took a running leap and threw her full weight against him, and both of them went flying down the stairs. Kasumi heard herself scream but had no idea what came out of her mouth. When everything was over, she found herself at the bottom of the stairs. The man was half a flight above her, his body contorted into an awkward position. He looked like he was stuck and couldn't get up. He stared at her, apparently stunned and speechless, and then thrust his arms forward as if trying to grab her. It so enraged her, Kasumi started kicking him.

"Stop, stop! I didn't mean any harm," the man pleaded.

Down the hall a door opened and someone bellowed, "What the hell is going on! Don't you know what time it is? I'm calling the police."

Kasumi started to run. She didn't particularly like leaving her apartment unlocked but she had no choice. Behind her she heard a loud ka-thunk, ka-thunk, the sound of something heavy—probably the man himself—rolling down the stairs. As it was starting to get light, Kasumi hugged the shadows as she made her way to the station, and even though no one seemed to be following her, she walked round and round for some time. By 7:00 A.M., the station was filled with morning commuters.

Kasumi had met the man through a friend. He had pursued her aggressively until she finally agreed to see him. It was not a case of surrendering to passion so much as being worn down by his dogged persistence. But then he started bragging openly about being her lover, and it made her so uncomfortable she began avoiding him. He stalked her after work. Why was she so cold? Did she have a new boyfriend? Someone who bought her lots of presents and flashed his money around? That's what women like, isn't it, he sneered. Then he announced that he would divorce his wife and marry Kasumi. If she refused, he would tell everyone at her workplace about the affair she'd been having. As a married man with children, he should have been the one to worry about this kind of gossip. He claimed he didn't care, he was prepared to give up everything.

So Kasumi had agreed to meet him one last time, and a date was set for three weeks later. She had a few things she wanted to lay on the line herself. Little did she know how strange their meeting would be.

Straight off she told him she couldn't stand the sight of him. She never, ever, wanted to see him again. The man acted like he was mulling her statement over. He raised his head and said, "I'll consider your request. In the meantime, though, I wonder if you could lend me a bit of cash?"

"What the hell!"

"I've got to raise some money fast. You're the only one I can think of asking."

His uncle had just died and left his estate to the man's mother, but unless they could pay the hefty inheritance taxes, everything would go to the government. Of course, whatever his mother received would eventually be his. And if Kasumi married him, it would be hers, too. Everybody got something. Right now, though, the more she could lend him the better. Could she manage at least three million yen? He'd still be short but could scrape together the rest from other sources. He'd spent an awful lot of money on her, he wanted to remind Kasumi. Dating her had wiped out most of his savings.

"That's your problem," she said tartly. "I told you, I'm not interested in marrying you."

"Okay, don't marry me. But how about a loan? You'll see, I'll be able to pay you back with interest."

She'd never heard anything so ridiculous. The man closed his eyes and let his head droop forward lower and lower onto his chest. Finally he covered his face with his hands and began to weep out loud, his shoulders trembling. Although Kasumi was sure he was faking it, the sound of his half-smothered sobs nonetheless gave her the creeps.

"This is the end for me. I'll never recover after being treated like this. You've destroyed a grown man. How does it feel? Does it feel good?"

"I told you to leave me alone," she replied coldly.

The man abruptly stopped crying. "I'm telling you, I'm desperate!"

For a full hour, they sat glaring at each other in stony silence.

Time passed, and Kasumi didn't hear from him. What a relief that was! After making such a fool of himself, he was clearly ashamed to show his face. Kasumi acknowledged that she had only herself to blame for jumping into an affair like that with a virtual stranger. Then, just as she had almost forgotten about him, she got a phone call late one night. How much was she willing to lend? the man asked, picking up just where he had left off.

"Not a single yen!" she cried, "Don't ever call me again!"

"You said you didn't want to see me," he muttered. "I thought it was okay to call."

"Well, the sound of your voice makes me sick, too!" she yelled in disgust. The man hung up.

The following night the phone rang again, only this time there was silence on the other end when she picked it up. What an idiot! Presumably this was because she'd said she hated his voice. After that, the phone rang every night, usually just around bedtime. If Kasumi didn't pick up the receiver, the ringing could go on for as long as thirty minutes. Soon she began to have trouble sleeping. Until the phone rang she was too anxious to sleep, and after it stopped she was so furious she was wide awake. What had she done to him, she asked herself in those sleepless hours, to deserve this kind of revenge. Had she been so awful? Granted it had been wrong to let him take her out when she didn't like him very much, but she'd been a little afraid of crossing him. In the end, she'd been stupid to let herself be dragged into an affair with someone she didn't want.

He called her at work, introducing himself as Kasumi's fiancé.

"It's a crank call, just hang up," Kasumi told her co-worker in the small company where she was employed as an office clerk. "I don't have a fiancé."

After getting off the phone, the co-worker came over to Kasumi. He was obviously very curious.

"I'm supposed to tell you that he wants to discuss the matter of a loan and you can expect a visit soon."

"I have no idea who the hell he is," she said.

"I see. No wonder it sounded fishy. This must be the latest kind of telephone scam. There are lots now. Once they get you on the phone they won't stop talking and before you know it they've tricked you into buying something. Later you get an invoice in the mail demanding payment or else."

"I didn't know that."

"Never utter the word 'yes' on the phone. Even 'uh huh' is dangerous. They can say you consented."

Kasumi couldn't help thinking what a perfect line of work that would be for a certain someone. As far as she knew, though, the man was legitimately employed as an English teacher either at a junior college or a prep school.

"I don't think it's that kind of call," she said.

Clearly disappointed, Kasumi's co-worker started walking away but not before advising her to be on guard anyway.

It was when she went home that very evening that Kasumi found Yamaguchi's change-of-address postcard in her mailbox. They'd met at a different company when both of them were starting out, and Kasumi had taken an instant liking to him. He seemed smart and capable. Later for different reasons they each ended up changing jobs and Yamaguchi went into publishing. Over time they lost touch.

According to his postcard, Yamaguchi had moved to the working class district of Shitamachi in eastern Tokyo about a year ago. Kasumi lived on the opposite side of the city. She never went to Shitamachi, which always seemed very far away, but the more she thought about the distance, the more appealing it seemed. Suddenly she wanted to visit very badly.

She went outside and immediately called Yamaguchi on the nearby pay phone. Ever since the man had begun harassing her, Kasumi had come to hate the telephone in her room. She didn't even like to touch it. If the phone rang, she just let it ring on and on. Sometimes she got so mad she threw things at it. As luck would have it, Yamaguchi was in and they had a nice long chat. When she said she wanted to come over, he sounded genuinely pleased. Not wanting to seem too forward, Kasumi explained that she was looking for a new place and hoped he could give her some advice.

"Of course, I can't afford an expensive new condominium like yours," she added.

"I'd be glad to do what I can, but I don't think I'll be much help. My place is not worth as much as you might think. The truth is it's haunted."

Kasumi could hardly believe her ears. Yamaguchi had never struck her as the superstitious type. Then again, her own telephone was "haunted" in a way, wasn't it? Maybe Yamaguchi had a similar kind of "ghost."

"Is your ghost a woman?" she asked.

"You're very perceptive."

"What exactly does she do?"

"Not much really. Sometimes I can hear her sobbing. Sometimes she slams the door. I think she's trying to scare me."

"She's angry with you."

"I suppose so. I don't normally talk about this, you know."

Yamaguchi had become engaged last fall after meeting someone through an *omiai*. He'd bought the new apartment for them to live in even though it cost more than he could comfortably afford. When the engagement was subsequently broken off, he ended up moving in alone. Given the circumstances, he hadn't felt like sending out change-of-address announcements. Then, this past summer, he heard that his former fiancée had been killed in a traffic accident. Shortly afterwards, the ghost began appearing.

"I can't see why she should hate me so much, but quite frankly I never could figure out what went on in her head."

Just before the wedding, Yamaguchi's fiancée started complaining that the apartment he'd bought was too small. Couldn't he get his parents to give them more money for a bigger place, she demanded. It might have been forgivable if she'd offered to help in some way herself, but as it stood, her attitude turned him right off. The thought of spending the rest of his life with a woman like that made Yamaguchi head straight to the go-between and call the marriage off.

"Aren't you glad you didn't get married?" Kasumi said after hearing his story. "Anyone who would want to come back and haunt you after death is not someone you could ever have understood."

How would the ghost feel if another woman came to the apartment? Would she try to attack her rival?

"Maybe you should come over and test it," Yamaguchi suggested. "You're still single, aren't you?"

"Sort of," Kasumi replied without elaborating.

The visit was arranged for the coming Sunday, but the plan was preempted by Kasumi's "ghost" on Friday morning.

It was the phone. It had been ringing all night and then started ringing again just before six o'clock. She was groggy from lack of sleep. Perhaps she'd reached the limit of what she could take. Perhaps talking to Yamaguchi the night before had given her courage. Instead of ignoring it as usual, she picked up the receiver.

Something had snapped inside, and though her mind was spinning around vacantly, her body was making preparations for battle. She got dressed, strapped on her waistpouch, and put the hunting knife she had purchased earlier inside. She loosened the fastener so the knife was ready to draw at a moment's notice. It was a nightmare: she would kill him if necessary—she didn't know how but she would. Push him out the window or stab him in the guts.

She thought about what Yamaguchi said when she'd asked him why he was ready to marry someone he didn't have anything in common with.

"I suppose I didn't think it mattered. I thought I could live with anyone as long as it wasn't someone I hated. I guess my fiancée sensed this and didn't feel too great."

Kasumi sometimes slept with men she didn't particularly care for just because she wanted to be held, and look at the mess she was in now. She didn't know whose fault it was—hers or that man's—but it was certainly true that when people felt they were being ridiculed or despised, it brought out the worst in them. No doubt Yamaguchi's fiancée came to hate him and it made her say awful things. Kasumi had dated a man she couldn't stand, and because he was hurt, he had turned into a monster. If he hadn't met her, he might have gone through his entire life without ever revealing that side of himself. Kasumi hated him because she'd let him touch her body, and her feelings towards him had, in turn, fueled his desire to make her suffer.

That morning she was so consumed with loathing that violence seemed a welcome release. But the man had been awake all night, too, and it seemed that both of them were feeling cornered and desperate. When Kasumi shoved him down the stairs, she was surprised at how little resistance he put up. Afterwards she thanked her lucky stars she hadn't killed him. Trust a man like that to come back as a ghost and persecute her for an eternity.

Going over these things in her mind, time went by without her noticing it. She fell asleep in Yamaguchi's bed before he came home, and when she woke the next morning, he had already left for work. She spent another day alone in his apartment. It was comfortable here, and she didn't feel like going home anymore.

In the end Kasumi married Yamaguchi. It happened so naturally, they could only laugh about it. They continued to live in the same apartment, which, although small—only two rooms and a kitchen—didn't feel particularly cramped for a childless couple. Yamaguchi complained about his busy workload—he usually left at 9:00 in the morning and didn't return until the middle of the night—but basically he was still the same straightforward, unpretentious guy Kasumi had known when they had worked together. At home he was cheerful and didn't expect her to wait on him. They got married when Yamaguchi expressed his hope that Kasumi would stay a long, long time. She was already a fixture in his apartment, and besides, she appeared to have driven away the ghost.

After getting married, Kasumi quit her job because Yamaguchi preferred that she stay at home. Otherwise the ghost might return, he joked. Kasumi didn't exactly believe in the ghost story, but didn't discount it entirely. If such a hard-headed materialist like Yamaguchi believed in it, there must be something to it, she thought, although it struck her as exceedingly odd that the ghost did not come out when she was alone. After all, if the ghost's objective was to make Yamaguchi suffer, wouldn't it make sense to torment his new wife? And if the ghost still loved Yamaguchi, you'd think it would try to scare Kasumi away so it could have him all to itself. This ghost didn't make any sense.

With no children and a husband who made few demands, Kasumi had a lot of time on her hands. There wasn't even a ghost to distract her. She should have taken up a project or enrolled in a course, but instead she simply did nothing. Sometimes she could spend a whole day just listening to the sounds outside. Small wonder that when the weather was rainy, wild or windy, she was overcome by nervous tension and started thinking about the ghost. What did the ghost think of her life with Yamaguchi, she would wonder, her mind spinning in circles. For that matter what would her former lover think of her life with Yamaguchi? The mere thought of the man made her furious, but curiously enough, thinking about Yamaguchi's ghost had a calming effect. She was just an ordinary, boring housewife now, she told Yamaguchi, but there'd been a time when someone had pursued her like a madman. People could get very obsessed, her husband agreed. In one way or another, they owed everything to the ghost.

Nothing like what happened before would ever happen again, she was sure, but if it did, she resolved not to run away in a panic. She'd stand her ground and make the man really suffer. What she'd done before was pathetic—shoved him a bit and then turned tail.

Her only consolation was that she hadn't lent him any money and she hoped that he'd lost the inheritance. Of course, she couldn't be sure that it hadn't all been a ruse to make her feel bad.

Even years later the feelings of desperation that had made her ready to kill were still inside her. She knew she was fully capable of violence if she ever met the man again, so she prayed their paths would never cross, not even by accident. Nonetheless she took good care of her knife.

Over the next several years, the area where they lived was completely transformed. New buildings popped up in once empty fields and old ones were torn down one after another. About the only thing that didn't change was the bright red paint on the guardrail bordering the expressway, which was visible from their apartment window. Traffic that used to move fast on the highway now traveled at a snail's pace.

Ito Drugs was closed for the fourth day in a row. Something she'd heard before made Kasumi worry that the store might be closing for good. The Itos had opened their store around the same time that Yamaguchi had bought his condominium, and Kasumi knew her husband was fond of the pharmacist, who'd given him a lot of advice when he was a bachelor. Kasumi tried to give the drugstore as much business as possible, buying household supplies as well as pharmaceutical goods. Even if it was a little more expensive, the service was good, and Kasumi frequently won practical things, like potatoes, in their promotional draws. Mr. Ito was from Hokkaido, so Hokkaido potatoes were a favorite prize.

Furthermore Kasumi still needed to buy medicated cream for Athlete's foot from time to time. It was as if that pig-headed man had burrowed right under her skin. The condition was chronic and stubbornly refused to go away completely.

Mr. Ito worked in the dispensary in the back, filling prescriptions, and his wife, Ayano, looked after the customers out front. When Yamaguchi and Kasumi went to the store together for the first time, Ayano remembered her. The couple had opened their own drugstore after Mr. Ito retired from a big pharmaceutical company. Although they lived far away in the west end of the city, they rose early every day to commute to their shop. Ayano didn't drive and if she didn't get a ride with her husband it took over two hours to come by public transit. I can't afford to get mad at him, she used to joke.

About a month ago when the store was still open, Kasumi had noticed how pale Ayano looked. It turned out that their landlord was trying to evict them.

"We might have to close the store," Ayano said, a troubled look on her face. "The landlord wants to sell the land. We've been here for seven years and people have finally gotten to know us. I don't know what will happen now. My husband is looking around at other locations, but it's a problem when you don't own the land. If only he'd let us buy it."

Kasumi had been married for six years.

"It's not fair to do this to you without any warning," Kasumi said. "Why don't you file a complaint with the business bureau?"

"We don't know how to fight something like this. We'd never win."

"But it's better to fight than to take it lying down."

The drugstore occupied the northeast corner of a concrete parking lot, and the landlord refused to sell unless the Itos bought the entire plot of land, including the parking lot. As she passed by the deserted store, Kasumi recalled that recent conversation. So things probably hadn't worked out after all, she thought.

However, the store did open once again. When Kasumi went

inside, she found Ayano all alone dusting the shop's stock. She turned around with a start when Kasumi started to speak.

"You were closed a long time."

"Oh, Kasumi-san."

"I'm so glad you're open again. How have you been?"

A shadow darkened Ayano's face as if she were struggling over what to say.

"Unfortunately I'm going to have to close the store again for a while. My husband just had surgery. He'll be hospitalized for at least a month."

"I didn't realize he was ill."

"Everything was very sudden. I'm sorry for the inconvenience."

"Don't be silly. You must be worried."

Thinking that Yamaguchi would surely want to pay a visit, Kasumi asked for the name of the hospital.

"No, no, that's not necessary," Ayano said, refusing to tell her. "The hospital is near where we live, out in the west end. It's too far away for you."

Later that night Kasumi told Yamaguchi what she'd learned.

"First an eviction notice, now an operation," he sighed. "What a crisis! The hospital bill must cost a fortune."

"Don't you think you should pay a visit to the hospital?"

'No. What would be the point? There's nothing I can do."

Kasumi recalled Ayano's pale haggard face. Even about the eviction, Yamaguchi sounded so cold and indifferent.

"It depends on the contract," he said. "If there's no protection clause in their contract, there's nothing they can do. Of course, they can try going to court if they want. Nowadays the landlord doesn't always have the upper hand."

Just before going to sleep, Yamaguchi stared up at the ceiling. "I guess I owe Mr. Ito a lot. It sounds awful what he's going through." He paused. "Believe me, if I thought that visiting him in the hospital would really make a difference, I'd go as many times as it takes." He glanced at Kasumi to see her response.

All of Kasumi's sympathy was for Ayano and her plight, and she often forgot to think about Mr. Ito. It would be enough if Yamaguchi, as a fellow male, worried about him. She felt that men were unknowable, and worrying about them wouldn't help. She never concerned herself with Yamaguchi's health or whether he worked too hard, and while she might be anxious about her own future, she didn't give his a second thought. Here she was, a married woman without the slightest intention of divorce, and yet ... well, it somehow didn't seem normal.

While these thoughts kept her wide awake, beside her Yamaguchi slept like a baby. Outside it was windy and the noise of the traffic sounded louder than usual. Well, what would happen if Yamaguchi got sick? What if they had to get a divorce? Once she started thinking like this, her head felt hollow inside.

The drugstore never reopened. Closed due to unforeseen circumstances, a notice pasted to the store's metal shutter read. Eventually the notice was blown away by the wind.

About a month later on a rare Sunday evening when Yamaguchi wasn't working, he accompanied Kasumi to the local supermarket. On their way home, they saw an old woman trudging wearily in their direction. "Look, Mrs. Ito!" Yamaguchi exclaimed. She'd aged almost beyond recognition.

"I wonder if she's reopened the store? Why would she be here on a Sunday?" Kasumi said.

"Let's find out." Yamaguchi called her name.

Ayano raised her head in surprise. As soon as she recognized Kasumi and Yamaguchi, she stopped and waited for them to catch up to her. Her eyes were red from crying and her whole face was puffy and swollen.

"It's been very hard, hasn't it. How is your husband?" Yamaguchi knew how to deal with people and could be good in situations like this. But tears welled up in Ayano's eyes and began rolling down her cheeks.

"What's wrong? I'm so sorry. Have I said something I shouldn't?" Flustered, Yamaguchi exchanged looks with Kasumi. Ayano wiped her eyes with the handkerchief she clutched tightly in her hand.

"When I see people I know, I fall apart and can't help crying," she said haltingly. "My husband died a month ago."

She pressed her handkerchief to her eyes again, and Yamaguchi hung his head low in silence. Of course, she'd given up the store.

Several years later the drugstore continued to remain unoccupied, and Kasumi couldn't help thinking the landlord hadn't had any intention of selling. All he'd wanted to do was evict the tenants.

"He probably can't find a buyer. The economy's bad," Yamaguchi said.

"But the stress of being driven out made Mr. Ito so sick it killed him. Don't you think someone should pay for that?"

"Maybe so, but where's the proof? Just how far do you think you'd get."

Yamaguchi's voice had a sarcastic tone that made Kasumi so mad she stopped talking to him, but he didn't seem to notice. Eventually the pharmacist and his wife ceased to be a topic of conversation.

One day a bulldozer demolished the drugstore, leaving a huge messy pile of ruins on the lot. A big piece of the drugstore's distinctive yellow and brown checkered linoleum was stuck at the top of the concrete heap where it flapped in the wind and rain, slowly disintegrating. Every time she looked at the peeling linoleum fragment, Kasumi was reminded of Ayano's face. The lot was soon overgrown with weeds—it wasn't even being used as a parking lot anymore—but the battered linoleum was a clear reminder of the drugstore that had once stood there.

In fact it wasn't until a condominium was built on the site a few years later that Kasumi finally discovered who the landlord was. It turned out to be their landlord, who, because he lived in their apartment building, was someone Kasumi said hello to all the time.

"Oh, I knew that," Yamaguchi said flippantly. "I didn't think it was worth mentioning. He owns almost all the land around here."

Kasumi was so stunned she was speechless.

As soon as the condominium was completed, the landlord and his family moved into their new, larger quarters. Not too long afterwards, a rumor began circulating that the building was haunted and that late at night you could hear the sound of someone sobbing. It was hard to find tenants.

When Kasumi told Yamaguchi about the rumor, he concluded the ghost had to be his ex-fiancee. "I'll bet she got confused and went to the wrong building."

"It's not your ghost," Kasumi said. "It's Mr. Ito."

Yamaguchi glared at her.

At Kasumi's insistence, they went over to look at the new building one night. It appeared deserted, dark and unlit except for the top floor where the landlord lived. Tiptoeing into the lobby, they strained their ears and listened hard. It was dead quiet. Yamaguchi cupped his hand behind one ear dramatically. "Can't you hear it? Someone's here! We better not hang around too long." He pulled Kasumi outside by the arm. She didn't know if he was just trying to scare her. She couldn't hear a thing.

On their way home, they passed a man and a woman, both tall, lean and youthful. But when their faces were visible under the light of the streetlamp, they didn't look very healthy. The couple was in the middle of having an argument.

"I've had enough!" The woman spoke sharply, averting her face from her partner. The man glared hard at the woman's nape.

"Do you suppose they live in the new building?" Kasumi turned around to look.

"Impossible."

"How can you be so sure?"

"They're headed for the public bath. Didn't you see they were carrying towels and soap."

As she watched the couple walk away, Kasumi felt a shiver run down her spine. One day, she felt certain, that woman was going to want to kill her partner.

"Uh oh. I was wrong," Yamaguchi exclaimed.

They stood together and watched as the young couple disappeared into the new apartment building.

∾

Dream Bug

The warm weather continued unabated. Coaxed out of his boarding house room by the bright blue sky, Hideo set off for Asakusa. His January second term finals were over, and the university had shut down completely for entrance exam preparations. This break was Hideo's last opportunity to really relax and take things easy. As soon as the new academic session began in April, he would have to start cramming for the company employment tests.

Until now he hadn't had a moment to catch his breath. It wasn't just that his exams came right after the New Year's holidays, he felt like he'd been rushing nonstop for months on end. At long last it was calm again, like the stillness after waves recede.

Hideo was headed for Uncle Katsuzo's coffee shop on the edge of the old Asakusa district. After Katsuzo died last fall, the shop was locked up just as it was, and Hideo, entrusted with the key by his father, was supposed to "keep an eye on things." He'd been curious enough at first that in November he made several trips, but the shop was far away and getting there involved several train and bus transfers. Once he'd stopped going, it was hard to start up again, and during the entire month of December he managed to go only once, just before returning home for New Year's. Today's visit in late January would be his first since coming back to Tokyo. It wasn't as if there was anything he actually had to do at the shop.

As soon as he set off, Hideo found himself thinking of the woman. He couldn't think of Katsuzo without the hazy image of the woman's face popping into mind, and he realized that for a long time he'd been repressing his desire to see the shop. Although he'd only caught one fleeting glimpse of her, the woman seemed to be lodged permanently in a forlorn corner of his memory, like something that had accidentally been left behind.

Over New Year's, a bigger crowd of relatives than usual had gathered at Hideo's family home. Not surprisingly, the main topic of conversation had been Uncle Katsuzo. All the brothers and sisters in the large extended family had something to say, squabbling among themselves over what they remembered of the dead man. All except Hideo's father, the eldest of the siblings, who stood by himself observing these proceedings in grim-faced silence. The sour look on his father's face wasn't new, however. He'd been looking like that for some time, for many months before Katsuzo died.

The past year had been a disaster for the farm. Hideo's family had farmed for generations, and although it was no longer the sole source of income, they continued to tend rice paddies, vegetable fields, and fruit orchards. But last year's perverse weather conditions—dry, blistering heat in the spring, an extremely short summer, and then a cold, wet autumn—meant the vegetables didn't grow and the fruit was small and sour. Most of what little they managed to harvest could not be sold. Who could blame Hideo's father for being in a foul mood.

Hideo had stayed in Tokyo that summer working at a part-time job. It was better than looking at his father's glum face day after day. But the weather in Tokyo wasn't normal either. By mid-July, when the rainy season would normally be over, it still hadn't rained a drop to speak of. Then, once the Weather Bureau officially pronounced the end of the "rainy season," like a bad joke it suddenly began pouring for days on end, forcing the meteorologists to hastily revise their forecasts. August was so cold and rainy people shivered in their short-sleeved clothing, and when it was time for classes to start again, Hideo felt there hadn't been a real summer at all. Autumn brought typhoon season. Everyday there were torrential downpours.

The day Hideo's father learned of Uncle Katsuzo's death and had to rush to Tokyo, it had been raining cats and dogs. Memories of Katsuzo seemed to be influenced by the endless depressing rain.

"As a youngster, Katsuzo was always in a daze, like he was half-asleep," Hideo's father said. "He was the most wishy-washy kid you could imagine! Whenever it rained, he would have nightmares and wake up sobbing. 'Don't be such a damned sissy!' Father would yell. He and Katsuzo never got along. For that matter, Katsuzo never got along with anyone in the family."

The rain didn't let up until the end of autumn, long after Hideo's father had finished tending to Katsuzo's affairs and returned home. But nothing could dispel the damp chill, and even when the sun shone, the weather refused to get warm. The cold, dry winds that were the harbingers of winter arrived a month earlier than usual. Then, in December, just as everyone was bracing for more cold weather, the temperature started to rise and the winds turned warm and clammy. After several failed predictions, the Weather Bureau finally announced it would be an unseasonably mild winter.

Day after day it was warm. Of course warm weather was preferable to cold, but such unnatural reversals in climate stirred up the emotions and upset the normal rhythm of life.

To Hideo the bustling activity around Asakusa Station felt like clouds of dust. Practically holding his breath, he hurried straight for the bus stop. Each time before coming here he thought how nice it would be to take a leisurely stroll through the lively shopping and entertainment district, but as soon as he arrived, it was always the last thing he felt like doing.

Getting off the bus at the fifth stop, Hideo stood facing Katsuzo's coffee shop. One glance was enough to know that the building had been deserted for some time. The sign was gone, and the shop had the seedy rundown air of an abandoned business. Although it was located in front of a bus stop, the coffee shop itself seemed virtually invisible.

Instead of going inside, Hideo walked back to the intersection and turned down the narrow street leading towards the river. He continued a short distance until he reached a dense patch of bushes which, although it was only January, were covered with blossoms that had just started to open. In a few days the bushes would be in full bloom. When Hideo had discovered these plants on his last visit in December, he'd wondered if they were Japanese quinces. But his botanical knowledge was limited and without seeing the blossoms he couldn't make a definite identification. He'd been waiting, and now he knew for sure. There was no mistaking the quince.

Hideo had made his discovery of the quince bushes on his way to Sakurabashi, a pedestrian bridge over the Sumida River that he'd read about earlier in the news. It was while looking at a map of the area that he realized the bridge was directly behind Katsuzo's shop. The road on which the coffee shop was located ran parallel to the north-south flowing Sumida River. From this road there were a number of narrow dead-end alleys leading directly back to the river. Hideo had begun walking down the closest alley and was almost at the riverbank when he suddenly came upon his quince bushes—about twenty or more altogether—planted in a dense row to form a hedge, a natural fence. The alley ended at a stone stairway that led up to the high river embankment. The Sakura Bridge was only a few meters to the left.

Very few bridges were for pedestrians only and, as far as Hideo could tell, this one was used as much for recreation purposes as for getting from one side of the river to the other. Designed in a crisscross "X" shape, the bridge had a large circular flowerbed in the middle where the lines of the "X" intersected. As they would at a park or garden, people gathered in relaxed groups, some seated on the edge of the flowerbed, others leaning against the clear plastic railings. Down below on the riverbank, people walked their dogs and children flew festive New Year's kites. Directly across on the other side of the river, Hideo could see Sumida Park, a dark mass of greenery. The expressway ran along the opposite bank hugging the shore except for one part that jutted out over the river. Standing in the narrow alley, it was impossible to see the river itself because the embankment was too high and a large white building, an athletic center, blocked his view. Compared to all the activity on the bridge and along the riverbank, here it was eerily hushed and deserted.

During the Edo period the "alley" had been filled with water and served as a waterway for boats delivering people to the Yoshiwara red-light district. Afterwards the canal was drained, filled in with dirt, and vegetation planted. A pile of crumbled stone remains was all that was left of the old bridge that had once stood here, its name inscribed on one of the old stone pillars toppled over on its side. It was as quiet and still as lying at the bottom of a deep ditch. Although a strong wind off the river swirled high above Sakura Bridge, in the spot where Hideo was standing, the breeze was so gentle it barely ruffled the flower petals. The stone wall to the south formed a protective barrier against which the western sun cast a glow over the fluttering blossoms.

Far from shining radiantly in this spotlight, however, the small fleshy petals of the quince looked dirty. They seemed to be coated with a brown film, perhaps the residue of microscopic particles of soil carried from the riverbank by the wind. Hideo rubbed his fingertips lightly on one of the petals, but the dirt seemed to be baked on and wouldn't come off. The flowers were mixtures of white and a dull shade of red, and the way the two colors blended together gave the blossoms a mottled appearance that made them look dark and heavy. From the bridge overhead, Hideo's ear caught the intermittent sound of a cassette radio, but strain as he might, he couldn't make out the tune. Every so often a few bars would float teasingly in his direction, only to be snatched away by the wind. The petals seemed to sway in time to the music, as if it were a song they knew from memory.

In front of the coffee shop, the wide busy road was filled with traffic, but hardly anyone walked on the street. The small, shabby buildings nearby were mainly wholesalers or factories that doubled as warehouses. Everything looked dingy, drab and unfriendly, like decrepit old men who'd lost their zest for life. That was Hideo's first impression when he came here, and it stuck. Of course, he had never seen Uncle Katsuzo's coffee shop when it was open for business, but certainly in its present state, nothing could have blended more perfectly into the surrounding grayness of the street. The shop was so inconspicuous, the average person would walk right by without even noticing it. If he were looking for a cup of coffee, Hideo thought, he wouldn't stop here. He'd look for someplace more inviting.

After first looking both ways to see if anyone was coming,

Hideo pulled out his key and inserted it into the lock. The doorknob was gritty and the door itself, made of black-hued plastic, was covered with dust. Mud had splashed up onto the bottom half and dried in patches. Just inside the doorway, his father had tacked up one of Hideo's worn bedsheets to serve as a privacy curtain. He found it extremely unsettling to see the sheet he used to sleep in hanging there.

Slipping past the sheet, Hideo pulled the door shut behind him and suddenly felt a cold shiver. It was so still and so dark. It was like entering the body of a dead person.

He perched himself on a nearby chair and, breathing shallowly, turned around to get a good look at the shop's interior. What a dump! It was more like a dreary mock-up of a coffee shop than the real thing. Although the shop was narrow it was extremely deep, and these proportions only served to reinforce its cramped closed-in feeling. Yet within a few minutes, Hideo was also struck by a sense of the familiar—the faintest blush of a feeling—the feeling that after a long absence he had finally arrived home.

Hideo really didn't know the first thing about Katsuzo. Although they were related—he was his uncle, after all—they had hardly seen each other. All Hideo knew was that there was something about the faint odor he detected in the coffee shop that reminded him of the smell that pervaded the family storehouse, the storehouse where he used to play as a child and where he'd found those stacks of old photographs. The family farmhouse was over a hundred years old, big and rambling, with a traditional storehouse built beside the main structure. It might have looked impressive if it weren't so rundown, but now it was just another dilapidated old country house. Perhaps it had been in better shape when his father and Katsuzo were children.

When Hideo was small, the storehouse had been his favorite hideout, his own private playhouse. When he got older, he turned it into his study, eventually even moving in his bed so he could sleep there. The storehouse was full of old junk, and Hideo did whatever he wanted with anything he found there. One of the "treasures" he unearthed was a stack of candy boxes stuffed tightly with hundreds of old photographs, all pictures of flowers. He selected the ones he liked best and pinned the photographs over his desk. It turned out that he kept picking the same flower—the Japanese quince—although it was not until much later that he learned what the flower was called and saw the real thing. He had no particular interest in biology and couldn't remember the names of plants or tell them apart, but thanks to those photographs, he could now recognize the quince. Wherever he went, the flower inevitably caught his eye.

Hideo was vaguely aware that his partiality for the quince had something to do with the way the flower, especially its pale pink waxy petals, reminded him of the kind of girl he liked. Even now the flowers triggered images of young girls, their faces hot and flushed, arms wrapped tight around swelling breasts, lost in some passionate private rapture. So when he accidentally discovered the cluster of flowering quinces right behind Katsuzo's coffee shop, he couldn't help feeling as excited as if he'd just met the photographer himself. By this time, the association of the coffee shop with the storehouse and the photographs was so strong in his own mind that he felt convinced they were connected. Surely Katsuzo shared his love of the quince.

It was as if a mist were filling his head. For reasons he couldn't explain, he felt such an intimate bond with Katsuzo that everything—the coffee shop, the shadowy face of the woman— bore an eerie sense of déjà vu. He knew them from long ago. He saw his younger self, locked inside the storehouse, enthralled by those photographs. Odd as it was, he even sensed that he had been inhaling the vapors of the storehouse long before he was born.

The fleshy petals of the quince dissolved into the face of the woman, and Hideo, too, felt the intense loneliness of changing into a different person. His gaze was pulled farther and farther into the unseeable distance, and he felt afraid. Was Uncle Katsuzo standing at the end of his gaze? Was Katsuzo watching him from some invisible place far away?

Until Katsuzo died last autumn, Hideo didn't even know he had an uncle in Tokyo, let alone one who lived in a place like this. Perhaps Katsuzo was simply attracted to secrecy, secrecy like a dark hole that opened up in the heart of the city. Hideo knew that eventually the coffee shop would be sold and changed into something else, something more practical, and that then the hole would close as quickly as a bubble on the water's surface. Until that happened, what harm was there if Hideo tucked himself inside the tiny opening left by a dead man?

Instead of getting a regular job after graduation, why couldn't he run this coffee shop? Of course, it was just a silly fantasy. His father would never approve, and anyway there was no money to fix the shop up properly. When it came right down to it, Hideo had to admit he probably wasn't up to the task.

By piecing together snatches of conversation he'd heard at home over the years, Hideo tried to solve the mystery of what had caused Uncle Katsuzo to cut himself off from everyone in the family. It was a family custom to send all the young men to Tokyo to attend university, just as Hideo was doing now, just as his father had done before him. After graduation everyone returned to the country and got a suitable job, using family connections if necessary. Almost from the start, Katsuzo had fallen off this established track. After failing his college entrance exams, he went back to Tokyo a second time, ostensibly to attend a cram school. But although he was officially registered at school for a while, the family heard from him less and less until finally there was no communication at all. Whether it was part of an intentional plan or whether something had happened to prevent Katsuzo from contacting his family and coming home, nobody knew. Eventually everyone gave up on him in disgust. The family didn't even know where to send his living allowance.

Katsuzo's parents were livid! While Hideo didn't remember much of his grandparents because they both died while he was still in primary school, what he did remember vividly was their sternness. They weren't the type to dote on their little grandson, and Hideo in turn was terrified of them. Even as a small child he sensed that he had better keep his distance.

After the death of his grandparents, however, a man Hideo had never seen before began calling on the family. Surely that was Uncle Katsuzo. It was probably easier to come home after the position of family head had passed to Hideo's father who, despite a gruff outer shell, was a gentle man at heart. At least he wasn't prone to flying off the handle like his own implacable parents who were always in a pique about someone or something. Come to think of it, wasn't the reason Hideo began hiding in the storehouse to escape the sound of Grandfather's voice?

Nobody ever explained to Hideo that this stranger was his uncle. He was never introduced, no greetings were exchanged. It was only much later, after putting together bits of gossip, that Hideo came to his own conclusion—so that was Uncle Katsuzo!

Among the old stuff in the storehouse was an old-fashioned camera, presumably the one that had been used to photograph the flowers. Until Hideo got his own camera, he loved to play with that antique contraption with two lenses in the front that met at right angles. When he looked through the camera, images appeared upside-down. Through lack of care, the lenses were coated with a film of white mold, the images as blurry as if shrouded in a pale mist. Of course not a shred of evidence linked Katsuzo to the camera, the photographs, the family storehouse or the quince. Hideo had many other uncles, all of whom had also been born and raised in the same country house.

Katsuzo had breathed his last in a woman's apartment, a matter of no small concern to Hideo's father who was mortified and filled with rage at his brother for dying "in a place like that." He fretted about the woman, what "sort" she was, convinced she would come forward with all kinds of demands. Yet for all his curiosity, he was extremely reluctant to meet the woman. He didn't want to talk, he didn't want to share his feelings. Yet he somehow expected the woman to open up and tell him everything he wanted to know. It was asking for too much.

Small wonder that when he finally did meet the woman, the tables were completely turned and he ended up having to do all the talking. The woman had been Katsuzo's only employee at the coffee shop and surely also his lover. From her, Hideo's father had hoped to glean a few clues into what Katsuzo's life had been like. He learned absolutely nothing.

They say that when a person dies the meaning of his entire life will become clear to those around him, but in Katsuzo's case, even the fact of his forty-some odd years of existence seemed in danger of slipping into obscurity. Desperate to find out more about who his younger brother was, Hideo's father paid visits to the neighbors. He sifted through the entire contents of the coffee shop with a fine tooth comb, carefully reading every scrap of documentation he found from top to bottom. He picked up each and every little trinket or article of clothing and turned it over in his hand. But the harder he grasped, the more elusive things were. Hideo was enlisted to help in these "investigations," and he could see how terribly disheartening it was. Listening to his father speak so tentatively about Katsuzo was like listening to a different person. Not his father anymore but someone else's brother. The brother of a dead man.

"A whole lifetime and this is all that's left to show for it. What a total failure!" His father's voice was filled with sadness.

Those remarks struck Hideo as very unfair. After all, Uncle Katsuzo's life had been cut short in his mid-forties, scarcely a "whole lifetime." But he did not interrupt because he understood that his father was upset about other things. Instead of getting properly married, Katsuzo had taken up with a woman half his age. It wasn't just in business, his personal life was a shambles, too, and a heavy curtain of disappointment hung in the air. When the woman had begun ranting to the police that she was the one responsible for Katsuzo's death, Hideo's father had had to deal with this headache as well. But more than anything else, he was clearly frustrated at knowing so little about his own flesh and blood brother, a man who remained such an enigma.

All the relatives, including Hideo's father, were convinced that Katsuzo had run away in shame and desperation after failing his entrance exams. You can't do anything with a guy like that! A hopeless case! Whenever people started talking about Katsuzo, they recycled the same old phrases. No one had anything good to say about him, but because no one actually knew anything, the conversation would quickly turn to other topics. Even as an object of gossip, Katsuzo was a bore.

When Uncle Katsuzo visited the family home, he never once exhibited the slightest interest in Hideo, even though he must have understood that his nephew would eventually become the clan head. Katsuzo never smiled at him, never spoke to him, never asked the others "Oh, who is that little boy?" Instead he would cast a cold, hard, indifferent glance in Hideo's direction, as if looking at a complete stranger.

Now he was dead and all that remained was a dreary coffee shop so small and cramped it could barely fit ten customers. Needless to say, business had not been particularly good.

Still, Hideo reasoned, wasn't it to Katsuzo's credit that he had fended for himself since he was only eighteen, even managing to purchase his own coffee shop. It was a substantial legacy. But his father only shook his head quietly. According to the account books, if Katsuzo had lived another two or three years, he would have ended up forfeiting the shop.

"It's amazing he kept the place afloat as long as he did. In a perverse way you have to admire him."

"Yes, that's what I meant," Hideo persisted. "He managed to make a living just like anyone else." He cared less about defending Katsuzo than offering his own father some kind of solace.

Finally his father recounted the whole story. After Grandfather died, much of the family land was sold and the money divided among the brothers. Even though over half was already gone, the estate had once been huge, covering mountain forests and large tracts of farmland. There was still a lot of land, and like all the brothers, Katsuzo had received a very handsome sum, an amount large enough to purchase a small shop in Tokyo. The inheritance was converted into a coffee shop; now the coffee shop was all that was left. Put another way, Katsuzo hadn't made a single contribution to anything on his own.

"Well, what more could you expect. At least he didn't leave any debts."

Gazing into his father's eyes, Hideo saw his own tiny reflection trapped inside those terribly dark, deep, glistening eyes. His father was staring off into space somewhere far away. Had Katsuzo also been hiding all these years in a place just as black and bottomless? A place of mysterious darkness from which, Hideo's father feared, all kinds of catastrophe could erupt at any moment. With their speculations and gossip, the family back home did their best to fill in the hole Katsuzo had left behind.

"Thank God he didn't commit suicide or get killed in some accident. Still, what a pathetic way to go. Not much better than dying on the street like a bum."

Katsuzo had been frail and sickly by nature, so it wasn't really such a surprise that he should die relatively young. But suffering a fatal seizure in the woman's apartment was indeed unfortunate timing. As the police explained, shock and a sense of guilt made the woman become temporarily unhinged.

Eventually all the affairs were taken care of, except one. It was time for Hideo's father to pay a visit on the woman. She had been an employee, and it was important to settle the matter of her pay once and for all. Of course, he was also more than a little curious about what kind of woman had had an affair with his brother.

Hideo came along but when they reached the woman's apartment door, his father abruptly sent him away, saying, "Wait at the coffee shop." Meeting at a restaurant would have been preferable for it would have given him the upper hand, but the woman had refused outright. Now he found himself in the awkward position of having to call on her uninvited.

"Anyway, it's not a bad idea for me to have a look at the place where Katsuzo breathed his last," he rationalized. "You can tell a lot about a person from where they live."

Two hours later he returned to the coffee shop shaking his head in bewilderment. He immediately made Hideo fetch some juice, which he gulped down without saying a word. To Hideo's quizzical looks, he simply shrugged his shoulders.

"It's amazing—she's just like Katsuzo! As tight as a clam. She didn't tell me a damn thing!" He forced a bitter smile. Haltingly he described what had happened.

The cramped apartment was every bit as dreary as the coffee shop. The woman sat in formal seated posture on the tatami mat, neither moving nor speaking. She didn't even look him in the eye. It seemed less that she was reluctant to talk than that she simply did not know anything. At first he thought she might be afraid but then realized that she had drifted into a kind of trance, completely oblivious to his presence.

She had nothing to say about Katsuzo, nothing to say about herself. When asked what she intended to do, she looked confused and her expression seemed to crumble as if she might burst into tears at any moment. But she made no reply, letting the silence between them stretch on unimpeded. She looked like she had drifted off into her own world again.

The woman had no conditions, no demands.

"I asked her several times if I could help. I said I wasn't trying to blame anyone. But if she won't talk, I can't do anything. You know, if Katsuzo had been a woman, I'm sure that's exactly how he would have turned out. It's really pathetic."

Hideo was relieved to see that his father wasn't as angry at the woman as before. "Maybe you can do something for her. Find her a job or something," he urged.

"Impossible. I can't take responsibility for a woman I don't know."

Hideo fell silent. His father had spoken sharply, but his next words were in a gentler tone.

"Well, I suppose I should be grateful to her for helping me remember what Katsuzo was like. He wasn't such a bad guy. Just a mouse. A nothing of a person. Even if he were standing right in front of you, you wouldn't notice him. He and that woman were two of a kind. No wonder they liked each other."

Hideo had only caught a brief glimpse of the woman in passing, yet his impression had been entirely different. He didn't know how to express it, but he sensed in her both strength and an inner radiance. The woman's eyes had been focused sharply on something in the distance, her cheeks flushed crimson. Hideo had instantly thought of the hard, young buds of the quince. These were scarcely thoughts he could share with his father.

Yet his father also acknowledged her toughness. "Remember, she took care of herself before she met Katsuzo. I'm sure she'll manage on her own. Anyway, we're no substitute for Katsuzo, and she doesn't want anything from us. I give up trying to figure her out. The two of them—what a pair of yumenmushi!"

If he had never been able to understand his own brother, how could he expect in one short meeting to comprehend this woman. In the end, Hideo's father handled matters as he saw fit. Before returning home to the country, he paid a final visit to her apartment and forced her to accept a packet of money—a suitable sum—as "severance pay."

His father had work to do. He couldn't stay in Tokyo forever. Alone in his room again, Hideo mulled over the word his father had used to describe Katsuzo. Yumenmushi. What on earth did it mean? It had such a familiar ring he hadn't thought to ask at the time, but no matter how he wracked his brain he was unable to recall where he'd heard it before.

He wanted badly to see the woman again, but could think of no excuse. On his way to Katsuzo's coffee shop, he would gaze up at the building where she lived, and once inside the shop, he stared vacantly into space. Sometimes in the moments just as he was drifting off to sleep, he liked to pretend that he was waiting for the woman's arrival. Once while napping in the coffee shop he'd had a very strange—yet disturbingly realistic—dream. The door of the shop opened just a crack, and though he wanted to get up he couldn't move. Somebody was peeking inside. Although the figure was hidden in the shadows, Hideo knew it was a woman, knew it was Katsuzo's woman. He wanted to go up close and make sure but his body was weighed down as heavy as a stone. Shot with light from behind, the woman's hair shone golden. That was all there was to the dream, nothing more. He had no idea how long it took him to wake up but as soon as he opened his eyes he felt as if the metal chains that were holding him down suddenly dissolved.

Of course it wasn't real. The coffee shop was locked! Nonetheless Hideo couldn't resist actually opening the door and peering outside. Nobody. Even so, he was unsatisfied. Still half asleep, he wandered unsteadily all the way over to the woman's apartment. At last he had thought of an excuse for calling on her. He would say the neighbors had seen her near the coffee shop, and he was here to find out what she wanted. But he never saw her. When he rang the doorbell to her apartment, there was no answer.

He came back a few days later when he wasn't groggy with sleep, but again there was no response. This time he'd brought along some cups and other knick-knacks from the coffee shop which he intended to offer as mementos. He left them in a bag in front of the apartment door with a note, but when he checked the following day, they were still there.

Quite possibly the woman was no longer living in the apartment. Hideo was afraid to find out. Picking up the bag of cups and knick-knacks, he took it back to the shop, forced to acknowledge that the dream had been nothing more than that. Even so he remained hopeful that she might come. Surely, he reasoned, she had her own key to the shop. He couldn't forget the vision in his dream. Bathed in light from behind, the woman's body was outlined with a dazzling brilliance, this time quite unlike the quince. The dream kept drawing him back to the deserted coffee shop.

It wasn't so hard to see how a person might choose to cut off family ties, how he might prefer to live in isolation. Hideo understood. Katsuzo wasn't as weird as people said. In fact, the deeper Hideo burrowed into the coffee shop, the more he came to feel a kinship with his uncle. Maybe it really was possible to slip out of reach of the family's probing eyes. As strong as any desire he might have to reveal himself to others, deep down Hideo felt an equally overpowering urge to efface all vestiges of his existence.

In the end, what had Katsuzo been but just an ordinary man? He hadn't gone bankrupt, he hadn't left debts. He'd loved a woman who was like himself. Even Hideo's father had found some solace in these simple facts. Katsuzo hadn't been a burden, he hadn't caused trouble. He'd simply run out of life.

After returning to his room at the boarding house that evening, Hideo tucked his legs under the warm *kotatsu* and soon drifted off into sleep. He had an excruciating nightmare.

He was on a mountain. He didn't know where but the shape of the mountain looked familiar like someplace near his home. At the top of the mountain was a lone persimmon tree. Its leaves had dropped and the branches were bare except for one ripe red persimmon. From afar, a crow had his eye fixed on the fruit. The last remaining persimmon on the tree was an offering to the gods and no one was allowed to eat it. This had been the law since olden times. Eventually the fruit would drop off the tree naturally to be consumed by the earth.

The crow knew the traditions. Hungry as he was, he knew he had to resist. Was he really so hungry? Perhaps it was the sight of the ripe persimmon that whetted his appetite. He swooped deliberately low, lightly brushing the persimmon as he passed, and perched on a nearby branch to get a closer look. It looked like a completely ordinary persimmon. The crow became increasingly impatient.

"What's everyone so afraid of? Punishment, ha! I've never heard of anyone being punished."

He never stopped to think that no one had ever violated the rule. No, the crow was beside himself thinking about the ripe red fruit. Left as it was, it was only going to drop to the ground and rot.

"What a bunch of cowards! No one is going to be punished. I'll show you. Just watch!"

When he saw that everyone had dropped what they were doing to watch, the crow felt a bit nervous, but without hesitation he climbed high up into the sky. He was a tough, brave crow. In one impetuous dive, he headed at full speed straight for the persimmon and sank his beak into the fleshy red fruit.

"How's that! Look, nothing's happened." was what he intended to shout in triumph. But he couldn't speak! His beak was stuck fast in the middle of the persimmon. He flapped his wings wildly in an effort to pull free and, thrashing his body around, tore off all the surrounding branches. It was useless. The persimmon had a grip on his beak as strong as if it were the hand of the mountain god himself. Although the panic-stricken crow tried to apologize to all around, there was no response. The mountain returned to its former silence and stillness. The other animals kept their distance from the transgressor, eyeing him fearfully from far away. In his desperate struggle to free himself, the crow ended up losing all his feathers and snapping his bones. Exhausted and worn out, he finally lost consciousness. The following year, the crow's shriveled black corpse still hung from the tree, swaying in the wind. The persimmon tree never bore fruit again.

Hideo felt he had partly woken in the middle of his dream, forced to watch the rest in a state of semi-consciousness. His throat was parched, he felt dizzy. Was he that crow? Or was he one of those watching from afar? The dream wasn't clear.

Yumenmushi. Hideo repeated the word unconsciously. The weird dream had left him with a feeling of revulsion, stirring up a loathsome memory in the pit of his stomach. Now he remembered where he'd heard the word. It was his grandparents who had taught him about the yumenmushi, the dream bug. Although nobody knew exactly what it looked like, the yumenmushi was a bug that hid inside dreams. As long as those dreams were sweet, the yumenmushi was content—no wonder it was especially fond of little children. But as children got bigger and began having nightmares, the yumenmushi started to writhe and squirm. To eliminate those painful, ugly, dirty dreams that continued night after night, the dream bug ate them up.

It was okay to have other kinds of dreams, but bad dreams had to be devoured. And if you had too many bad dreams, your mind would soon be filled with holes chewed by the yumenmushi. Once it had eaten up everything, you could never dream again. You were spared having nightmares, but you lost the capacity to have good dreams too. Sleep was a long unbroken band of blackness. But the real terror of the dream bug's displeasure was in one's waking hours, for it sucked away all passion until living itself became just too much trouble.

Dirty boy! Behave yourself! Bad boys have bad dreams! No doubt this was the moral lesson his grandparents had wanted to impart.

Just like a yumenmushi! That's what his father had called Uncle Katsuzo. But what about himself? Wasn't Hideo one of the same?

The dream had left a sour aftertaste. He would examine his dreams closely from now on for signs of the dream bug, looking for those telltale pitch-black holes, so dense and so opaque. But what was the point, for how could he control his unconscious? He could only watch helplessly as his dreams were consumed.

Had Katsuzo been eaten alive by the dream bug? The woman, too?

Hideo stood up and shook his head hard from side to side as if to knock out the remnants of his nightmare. He felt slightly dizzy. Although he resolved that night to dream of the flowering quince, it was the image of the crow desperately thrashing back and forth, its beak stuck fast in the persimmon, that flashed through his mind yet again.

∽

CORNELL EAST ASIA SERIES

80 Mark Peterson, *Korean Adoption and Inheritance: Case Studies in the Creation of a Classic Confucian Society*

81 Yenna Wu, tr., *The Lioness Roars: Shrew Stories from Late Imperial China*

82 Thomas Lyons, *The Economic Geography of Fujian: A Sourcebook*, Vol. 1

83 Yu Young-nan, tr., *Park Wan-suh: The Naked Tree*

84 C.T. Hsia, *The Classic Chinese Novel: A Critical Introduction*

85 Chun Kyung-ja, tr., *Cho Chong-Rae, Playing With Fire*

86 Janice Brown, tr., *Hayashi Fumiko, I Saw a Pale Horse and Selections from Diary of a Vagabond*

87 Ann Wehmeyer, tr., *Motoori Norinaga, Kojiki-den, Book 1*

88 Chang Soo Ko, tr., *Sending the Ship Out to the Stars: Poems of Park Je-chun*

89 Thomas Lyons, *The Economic Geography of Fujian: A Sourcebook*, Vol. 2

90 Brother Anthony of Taizé, tr., *Midang: Early Lyrics of So Chong-Ju*

92 Janice Matsumura, *More Than a Momentary Nightmare: The Yokohama Incident and Wartime Japan*

93 Kim Jong-Gil tr., *The Snow Falling on Chagall's Village: Selected Poems of Kim Ch'un-Su*

94 Wolhee Choe & Peter Fusco, trs., *Day-Shine: Poetry by Hyon-jong Chong*

95 Chifumi Shimazaki, *Troubled Souls from Japanese Noh Plays of the Fourth Group*

96 Hagiwara Sakutarō, *Principles of Poetry (Shi no Genri)*, tr. Chester Wang

97 Mae J. Smethurst, *Dramatic Representations of Filial Piety: Five Noh in Translation*

98 Ross King, ed., *Description and Explanation in Korean Linguistics*

99 William Wilson, *Hōgen Monogatari: Tale of the Disorder in Hōgen*

100 Yasushi Yamanouchi, J. Victor Koschmann and Ryūichi Narita, eds., *Total War and 'Modernization'*

103 Sherman Cochran, ed., *Inventing Nanjing Road: Commercial Culture in Shanghai, 1900–1945*

104 Harold M. Tanner, *Strike Hard! Anti-Crime Campaigns and Chinese Criminal Justice, 1979–1985*

105 Brother Anthony of Taizé & Young-Moo Kim, trs., *Farmers' Dance: Poems by Shin Kyŏng-nim*

106 Susan Orpett Long, ed., *Lives in Motion: Composing Circles of Self and Community in Japan*

107 Peter J. Katzenstein, Natasha Hamilton-Hart, Kozo Kato, & Ming Yue, *Asian Regionalism*

108 Kenneth Alan Grossberg, *Japan's Renaissance: The Politics of the Muromachi Bakufu*

109 John W. Hall & Toyoda Takeshi, eds., *Japan in the Muromachi Age*

110 Brother Anthony of Taizé & Young Moo Kim, trs., *Kim Su-Young, Shin Kyong-Nim & Lee Si-Young: Variations: Three Korean Poets*

111 Samuel Leiter, *Frozen Moments: Writings on Kabuki, 1966–2001*

112 Pilwun Shih Wang & Sarah Wang, *Early One Spring: A Learning Guide to Accompany the Film Video February*

113 Thomas Conlan, *In Little Need of Divine Intervention: Scrolls of the Mongol Invasions of Japan*

114 Jane Kate Leonard & Robert Antony, eds., *Dragons, Tigers, and Dogs: Qing Crisis Management and the Boundaries of State Power in Late Imperial China*

115 Shu-ning Sciban & Fred Edwards, eds., *Dragonflies: Fiction by Chinese Women in the Twentieth Century*

116 David G. Goodman, *The Return of the Gods: Japanese Drama and Culture in the 1960s*

117 Yang Hi Choe-Wall, *Vision of a Phoenix: The Poems of Hŏ Nansŏrhŏn*

118 Mae J. Smethurst & Christina Laffin, eds., *The Noh Ominameshi: A Flower Viewed from Many Directions*

119 Joseph A. Murphy, *Metaphorical Circuit: Negotiations Between Literature and Science in Twentieth-Century Japan*

120 Richard F. Calichman, *Takeuchi Yoshimi: Displacing the West*

121 Fan Pen Li Chen, *Visions for the Masses: Chinese Shadow Plays from Shaanxi and Shanxi*

122 S. Yumiko Hulvey, *Sacred Rites in Moonlight: Ben no Naishi Nikki*

123 Tetsuo Najita & J. Victor Koschmann, *Conflict in Modern Japanese History: The Neglected Tradition*

124 Naoki Sakai, Brett de Bary & Iyotani Toshio, eds., *Deconstructing Nationality*

125 Judith N. Rabinovitch & Timothy R. Bradstock, *Dance of the Butterflies: Chinese Poetry from the Japanese Court Tradition*

126 Stephen Epstein & Kim Mi-Young, trs., *Yang Gui-ja: Contradictions*

CORNELL
East Asia Series

Order online at www.einaudi.cornell.edu/eastasia/publications